Tim Lawson

About the Author

DORIE MCCULLOUGH LAWSON is the author of *Posterity: Letters of Great Americans to Their Children*. The daughter of renowned historian David McCullough, she lives in Rockport, Maine, with her husband, the artist T. Allen Lawson, and their four children. *Along Comes a Stranger* is her first novel.

Along Comes a Stranger

Along Comes a Stranger

Dorie McCullough
Lawson

HARPER

NEW YORK • LONDON • TORONTO • SYDNEY

HARPER

A hardcover edition of this book was published in 2007 by HarperCollins Publishers.

ALONG COMES A STRANGER. Copyright © 2007 by Dorie McCullough Lawson. All rights reserved. Printed in the United States of America. No part of this book may be used or reproduced in any manner whatsoever without written permission except in the case of brief quotations embodied in critical articles and reviews. For information address HarperCollins Publishers, 10 East 53rd Street, New York, NY 10022.

HarperCollins books may be purchased for educational, business, or sales promotional use. For information please write: Special Markets Department, HarperCollins Publishers, 10 East 53rd Street, New York, NY 10022.

FIRST HARPER PAPERBACK PUBLISHED 2008.

Designed by Nicola Ferguson

The Library of Congress has catalogued the hardcover edition as follows:

Lawson, Dorie McCullough.
   Along comes a stranger / Dorie McCullough Lawson. — 1st ed.
      p.   cm.
   ISBN: 978-0-06-088475-8
   ISBN-10: 0-06-088475-4
   1. Bulger, Whitey, 1929—Fiction. Title.

PS3612.A933F57 2007
813'.6—dc22   2006049365

ISBN 978-0-06-088477-2 (pbk.)

08 09 10 11 12 ID/RRD 10 9 8 7 6 5 4 3 2 1

For Tim

Along Comes a Stranger

George and I hardly talk about the summer of 1995 anymore. I suppose the details have faded from our minds, but even more, I think we've just moved on, mostly. I can't remember the last time Lorraine mentioned it, and with Clara, it's hard to know how much she remembers, or how much she understood at the time. She was just turning seven years old then.

A few weeks ago Clara was looking for a childhood picture for her high school yearbook, and in a box among some photographs she came across a note. It was small and it was handwritten and it was signed simply, "Tom." With the piece of paper in her hand, she came to me full of questions. Of course she knew who Tom was, but now she wanted to know more. The look on her face was not one of apprehension or fear. No, her expression reminded me of the small child who asks eagerly, "Tell me about when I was little."

I didn't answer her. Instead, I went upstairs and pulled a box of pages from under my bed. I knew she'd probably understand best if she just read what I wrote down as soon as I could think clearly after it all happened.

chapter 1

Bear Creek Road
Hayden, Wyoming
1996

"You never really know about people," I remember my father saying when I was a little girl. And he was right. You don't. You never really know.

What happened to me and to my family a year ago, during a few weeks of the summer of 1995, was something I never expected. Who could have expected? It seems as unlikely now as it did then. I'm trying to write it all down, then maybe I'll be able to see what's important, what matters to me, and what doesn't. Maybe then I'll be able to explain it to Clara someday in a way that makes sense.

I once knew a boy named Jake who watched his best friend die. The two teenage boys were swinging from a rope into a lake. The friend let go before he was over the water, landed on a rock, and bled to death. All the bleeding was internal, so neither boy knew how serious the injury was. The point is that Jake was there when his best friend died. He was part of the death, and that's one of life's big experiences, one that most of us never have. With my aunt Joanie afterward, I said, "This will change Jake forever."

Without missing a beat, Joanie, who sees to the heart of things quickly, said, "And if it doesn't, he's an idiot!" Well, I'm not going to be an idiot.

I'm forty-one years old and I grew up in the East. My name is Kate Colter, Kathleen Louise Vaile Colter. George Colter is my husband, and our daughter, Clara, is about to turn seven. We've wished for more children, but it just hasn't happened. George is a paleontologist. He teaches at the community college and does fieldwork all over Wyoming. His specialty is the Eocene epoch, and he spends a lot of time in the southwestern corner of Wyoming at Fossil Butte. When people ask what I do, I say, "I'm at home with Clara," but I do have a part-time job; I just keep it quiet because I can tell my boss, Mr. Stanley, prefers it that way. Mr. Stanley is a well-to-do, elderly gentleman who keeps to himself, and I pay his bills and do the payroll for his Rafter T Ranch. As a sideline, I'm available if you have a horse (or a dog, or a sheep—no cows) that needs something extra—a wound needing regular bandaging, medication, and a clean stall, anything really. For this people usually pay me with money, but not always. Barter is alive and well here, and I've traded for almost everything from dental work, to fly-fishing equipment, to a year's worth of oil changes. I wish someone would trade for plane tickets or books, but that hasn't happened, either.

We live in Hayden, Wyoming, George's hometown, in a state so full of fossils it's a suitable home base for paleontological fieldwork. George and I met in New York City fifteen years ago while he was working at the Museum of Natural History and I was visiting a friend in Connecticut during my awkward, confused time right after college. We sat next to each other on the train and started talking. The day had turned from beautiful to cold and raw and I had no coat, and George, the Westerner and gentleman that he is, had a jacket to loan me. The next day I returned it to him at the museum, and the rest, as they say, is history. When he asked me to marry him, I knew I was saying yes to him, and yes to Wyoming. Like so many women, I'm here because of a man. There are girls who came with their families to dude ranches from places like St. Louis and Pittsburgh, fell in love with cowboys, and stayed; women who met their husbands back east at college and then came west with them; and gals who were here visiting for one reason or another, met the right guy, and just couldn't leave. With hardly any effort I can list women from eighty-nine years old on down who stay here for a man, but I can't think of a single man who's here for a woman.

My mother-in-law, Lorraine, lives in Hayden, too, and I'm lucky because I like her. She doesn't really know me, she just thinks I'm George's "nice wife from back east," and that's about it. It used to drive me crazy, but now I'm used to it. George is still bothered, but what can I do? George's father died years ago of kidney failure, and ever since, Lorraine has been the receptionist at Mountain Vision Ophthalmology. Lorraine knows what's going on in town and she doesn't care much about anything outside of town, unless, of course, it's on TV or in her *Country Woman* magazine. She's small and pretty, with fine features. Her skin is so even that it must have hardly seen the sun, and at sixty-four, her legs look better than mine. Anyway, it's important to mention her now because all that happened last summer began with her.

Before I get into the events of a year ago, I should explain my frame of mind at the time. Summer had come on strong, as it always does. So, so hot, and dry. It was the middle of July, midmorning, and I remember stepping out of the overly air-conditioned Albertsons grocery store. Pushing my cart to the truck, I could hardly see in front of me because it was so bright. The heat was too much already, hitting me from the sun above and the pavement below. At the far end of the parking lot there were more RVs than usual, probably because Rodeo was about to begin. Clara followed closely behind talking mostly to herself. Suddenly I was overwhelmed with a thought, a feeling really—Is this it? Is this all it's going to be? Just moving from one moment to the next, buying groceries, putting them away, worrying about paying for them, worrying about Clara's health, feeding the dog, knowing I'm lucky in my marriage and to have my daughter, driving my car down the road, being frustrated and then fine, talking on the phone, buying groceries again ... Could this really be all it is? Why is it that sometimes the world seems fascinating and sometimes I don't have the strength to care?

That's how I was thinking last year at this time. It was the next day I first heard the name Tom Baxter.

chapter 2

If you're used to living near the ocean, there is hardly a
thing lonelier than the middle of the country in summer.

Hayden is a quiet town, mostly, and I suppose not
that different from any small town in the West, or any
small town anywhere, for that matter. The main street
is wide and fairly attractive. It begins at the south end
with a beautiful, domed courthouse, the Old Courthouse, which is surrounded by lawns and mature cottonwoods and sits solidly on the top of a knoll. The town
park and pool are behind. Next to the Old Courthouse
is the flat-roofed New Courthouse, whose construction
and design, I hear, were the pride of the town in the sev-
enties. It's too bad because from the bottom of the hill,
you can hardly see the older building behind the new.
Main Street runs straight north and south and divides
the town into east and west sections. (We live east, out
of town, and Lorraine lives in town, up on the hill to the
west.) The buildings on Main are mostly brick or sand-

stone, and many are too big for today's purposes. Jamesons' New York Department Store, Up-Town Shoes, and Hayden Hardware have all shut down. To keep up appearances, the chamber of commerce and the Hayden Business Council make sure no storefront windows are boarded up or papered over; instead they're all used as display cases for other businesses. That way when you drive through town it doesn't look sad. Plenty of stores on Main are doing fine, like Mountain Sports, Reliable Computer, a restaurant or two, more than a few bars, the banks, a coffee shop, and a trophy shop. Somehow The Coin Shop holds on, too. At the north end, beyond low-slung motels and pawnshops, the truck stop, car washes, a bar or two with drive-up windows, convenience stores, the lumberyard, feed and ranch supply stores, and Wal-Mart, is the interstate highway.

Just before the interstate, railroad tracks cross and then run parallel to Main before they head east. Passenger trains used to stop in Hayden, but they haven't for a long time now, and the old depot has been turned into a pathetic pool hall. Burlington Northern coal trains, loaded at the mines outside town, roll through a few times a day and night blowing their whistles. They say it takes a whole trainload of a hundred cars to light Chicago for just one night.

The coal mines are strip mines, and for as long as anyone can remember, they've employed quite a few people, from drivers and welders to managers and accountants. The machines run, moving the overburden, extracting the coal, and supposedly reclaiming the land, twenty-four hours a day, three hundred and sixty-four days a year. The one day a year the mines close is October 15, the first day of elk season. Hardly anyone worries about the land because there is so much of it, and no one seems to have much use anyway for that barren, godforsaken stuff twenty miles north of town. George and I worry sometimes, I guess, but I shouldn't talk because we don't do anything about it.

Coal has changed Hayden recently in another way. A few years ago someone figured out a cheap way to flush out natural gas, methane, from the coal seams. Coal bed methane brings new people to town, and pump stations have popped up on the plains and hillsides all around the county. Some people are getting rich, some are seeing opportunity, and some are just getting frustrated and mad, all the kinds of things that happen with change.

To the west of Hayden are the foothills and then the mountains. The mountains are old, worn, and soft-edged, and I never get tired of looking at them. They look close, but it's more than an hour's drive to the base. The Great Plains, brown and dusty green in the summer, stretch out to the east. Storms come from both directions, but the thunderheads from the east seem the most dramatic. Maybe it's because you can see them approaching from so far away. Ranches of all sizes are in every direction.

Besides the miners and coal bed methane people, it seems to me that there are essentially four kinds of people who live here. No one likes to be categorized, I know, but this is just how I see it. There are those who keep it all going; the insurance agents, pharmacists, and state highway workers. They go to church, play in softball and bowling leagues, drink beer on Friday nights, ring the bell for the Salvation Army, and coach Little Guy Football. They don't usually drive fancy cars or indulge themselves in every available comfort as a matter of economics, yes, but also that's just how they are. Take air-conditioning, for example. Most people in Hayden don't have it. Sure, it's expensive to put in and to run, but even more than that the attitude is: Who really needs such a luxury when the summer is so short and it generally cools down at night anyway? They work and they live life as it is, and without complaints.

Then there are the fancy professionals, some who grew up here and return proud, and others who come from places like Denver and Chicago. They come for the mountains, the fishing, and "the way of life," but then they complain about the schools and pine for latte. They amuse themselves with Wild-Beast Feasts and the annual

Doctor-Lawyer's Ball. Many of them wear cowboy hats and boots, but I doubt they're very good in the saddle.

There are the ranchers, and there are a few real ranchers left—people struggling to make their living from cattle—and the families who run the dude ranches. And there is another set on the ranches, too, the middle-aged sons and grandsons of past generations of ranchers, who are now the managers of the private Western playgrounds of the ultra-rich. They know the land, they know the wildlife and how to hunt, they know how to pack a horse and break a colt, they know when to move the cows to the mountain and when to head for the vast feedlots of Kansas and Nebraska, and they know which bull to buy at the Billings stock sale. Their wives can cook at cow camp and feed a crowd at branding, but these ranch managers are not the self-sufficient men of Western myth. They're like corporate cowboy executives with fancy trucks and expensive guns, and they're employed by people who use farm subsidies and a tax-free state to maintain their wealth. Most of the time these ranch managers can live as they wish, close to the land and to the people they know, but when the bosses' little jets hit the Hayden landing strip, their true purpose, fun and entertainment, is clear.

Then there are those who fall into no real category. I can think of an artist or two, an opera singer, and a few divorcées escaping old lives and living now on I don't know what. A falconer lives on the edge of town, and you can sometimes see him standing in a field dressed in bedsheets. Most of his clientele is Saudi Arabian, and it's important that his birds get accustomed to the traditional Middle Eastern dress before leaving Wyoming. There are interesting people here, certainly. It's just in the fifteen years or so that I've lived here, I haven't quite figured out how to get my life connected to theirs. I'm not sure where exactly George and I fit in.

Last year, on July 12, the day after I had my thoughts in the Albertsons parking lot and the day before Rodeo began, we went to Lorraine's annual Omaha Steak Party. She takes the whole week of Rodeo off from work, always has, and she has her party on the Wednesday before the Rodeo events kick off. The funniest thing about Lorraine's party is that it's at three o'clock in the afternoon, and that makes George furious because it's the middle of the day. It's neither lunch nor dinner, and his whole day is interrupted. The party is mostly for family; sometimes friends and neighbors are there, too. Everyone, except for us, arrives right at three, or five minutes before, and the food is served promptly at 3:05. We try to be on time, but we usually show up at ten after or so, and Lorraine gives us a look. Last year was no different.

George had just gotten back two days earlier from a dig in Kemmerer, and he was downstairs in his woodshop working on Clara's birthday present. The basement is pretty much his—he has his office and fossil collection down there, and he divided off a separate room to be his woodshop. He says it's too small, but better than nothing, and last year before we went to Lorraine's party he was working on a little desk for Clara. That afternoon he was sanding away, hoping to be able to get at least two coats of varnish on before leaving again to go back to the dig.

I was behind the house, in the barn with Clara, checking on everybody and filling water buckets. Horses go through a lot of water in the heat. I had only two in the barn—a sorrel mare with a bowed tendon, and Timmy, a spotted pony who had been with us for a month and I knew would stay for a while. His owners bought a place up by the mountains and thought they'd gotten rid of all the barbed wire. But obviously they missed some, because they turned Timmy out and he came in the next day with a lacerated pastern. That bottom strand of barbed wire is a killer on horses. I think most people would have put Timmy down, but the Nicholsons' grandchildren adore him, so we're giving it a chance. Outside we had our old horse and two belonging to a lawyer couple in town who were away on a raft trip.

We had lost track of time that afternoon and headed for Lorraine's party late, again. I never seem to look at my watch when I should. We barreled down our dirt road, throwing up a huge dust trail behind us, and drove the five miles fast. After we drive the long, empty stretch of County Road 64, on our way to town we pass the community college where George teaches, a bunch of ranchettes with big garages, two trailer parks, and an old people's home. There's a sign on the right side of the road that makes me feel like laughing, or maybe crying, every time I drive by. It stands in front of a derelict shack of a house and reads, "Living My Dream—Crafts."

Main Street was empty as usual on a hot summer day, even though the biggest event of the town's year was less than twenty-four hours away. A few men in white cowboy hats ducked into doorways. Pickups and horse trailers were parked along the curb. Except for the flags and the windows painted with signs such as "Welcome Rodeo Fans" and cartoon pictures of busty cowgirls saying, "Howdy Pardner," Main Street looked about the same as it always does. The houses in the neighborhoods had their shades pulled to keep out the sun and heat. Hayden looks like it's in mourning all summer long.

Lorraine has lived in her house in Arapahoe Court subdivision since George was a little boy. It's a low, ranch-style house with light blue aluminum siding. Rosebushes line the foundation to the south and east, and a propped-up wagon wheel divides the driveway from the lawn. Wooden barrel planters filled with pink and purple petunias lead from the driveway to the deck. Her house is never anything but immaculate.

We turned the corner onto her street, and I was nearly bowled over by the biggest fifth-wheel camper I'd ever seen parked against the house. The top of the gooseneck was almost as tall as the peak of the roof. When I exclaimed over the camper, Lorraine, who was just coming out of the door, said, "Oh, honey, do you know you're the first person to notice it!"

When something major happens in your life and you look back on the days and weeks surrounding it, the details and little things you remember are sometimes strange—like snapshots in an album where the order sometimes matters and sometimes doesn't. Last summer is like that for me now, vivid moments standing on their own, the ordinary and the odd, all somehow connected in the end. In my mind Lorraine's party seems to be the beginning of it all because I first heard of Tom Baxter and also because the beginning of Rodeo is the time when these punctuated memories of mine start. If the memories of last summer were a necklace, I guess Lorraine's party would be the first bead—or maybe the loop end of the clasp.

Who could forget that enormous camper that turned out to belong to George's sister, Kelly, and her husband, Jim, who'd driven the four hours from Rapid City? Or Lorraine nearly going crazy over the "slide out" living room, and how she told me all about visiting the Jayco RV Headquarters once in Middlebury, Indiana, where the factory floor was so clean you could eat your dinner off it? But I also remember funny things like the name of her new, scented candle, Endless Summer, and the strange feeling I had walking in the front door of the house. Nothing had changed in the room, but I suddenly found myself feeling very sorry for a tiny Victorian settee. For as long as I've been going to Lorraine's house, the dainty little couch has been sitting oddly on the wall-to-wall baby blue carpet with its back resting against a faux paneled wall. The story is that it had come west with Lorraine's great-grandmother on the covered wagon. But that's it, that's the extent of the story. No one knows from where the couch, or the family for that matter, had come, except for "back east somewhere." Or why they stopped in Hayden. No one really knows anything. Where had it been, and why? Who made it? I tried for a bit to find out more, but I didn't get anywhere, either. So I remember myself at the beginning of Rodeo, at the beginning of a party, for a moment feeling sad and lonely for an old piece of furniture whose whole story had been reduced, to the satisfaction of everyone, to simply, "It came from back east on the covered wagon."

People connect with other people in the ways they can. Sometimes it's easy and sometimes it takes an effort. There are people who worry about it and there are those who don't. I worry, George doesn't. I try and George hardly makes an effort if it doesn't come easily. Lorraine, happy as can be, strikes up conversations all over the place. Whether she's making a connection with another person is something I don't think she concerns herself with one bit. Really, what is the point in worrying about that?

In my mind, the Omaha Steak Party went something like this: Clara and I looked at Lorraine's doll collection displayed in a lighted corner cabinet. We talked about a china figurine I loved at my grandmother's house and how she looked out the window from her bookshelf at the boats in the harbor. Clara thought she liked Grammy's (that's what she calls Lorraine) *Wizard of Oz* Dorothy best because of the sparkly ruby slippers and Toto. Lorraine overheard us talking and smiled a big, warm smile and said, "Clara, aren't Grammy's dolls just beautiful?"

Clara nodded.

"I just got Scarlett O'Hara last week." Then she turned to me, her thick, black, hot roller curls framing her face. "When I called they said she was sold out, but they'd put me on the wait list. Oh . . . I was heartbroken. So you can imagine how I almost fell over when the box arrived."

She kept talking as she headed for the kitchen. "You know, they're collectors' items. Snow White was my first. Oh … that was years ago and I have *no idea* what she's worth now, but I can guarantee it would be a pretty penny."

Over steak and macaroni salad, I did what I often do—I brought up George's work. I told everyone about what he was doing at Fossil Butte in Kemmerer. I explained how he was in charge of the research team and there were paleontologists and students from UCLA, Princeton, Kansas State, and the Smithsonian. Lorraine was beaming and nodding at me. After stuffing a lemon wedge into her Diet Pepsi can, she started rubbing George's shoulder affectionately. George, a bit uncomfortable, began to explain how they were all working in one-meter-square grids excavating fifty-million-year-old fish skeletons.

"Most of 'em are partial skeletons, but there are a few complete fish," he said. "Fossil Butte is part of the Green River Formation, and people have been finding fossils there for more than a hundred years and there are still hundreds of thousands to find. I study two species of fish, *Knightia* and the *Priscacara*. *Knightia* is related to the herring, but *Priscacara* has no modern descendants. Anyway, most of the fish preserved in what was Fossil Lake died of natural causes. But there are some layers in the sediment, we call them mass mortality layers, where it is clear that something changed and killed a lot of fish all at once. And that's what we're trying to figure out—why they died."

There was a silence in the room. My mouth was full, but I couldn't stand it, so I chewed fast and filled the void. "Do you have any theories about how they died?"

George knew I already knew the answer, but he humored me and explained to everyone at the table. I remember looking over at him as he spoke and thinking that his broad face was handsome and that his modesty was genuine. "Well, it could have been a sudden temperature change—this was all a subtropical climate then. Or it could have been a major blooming of algae that kept oxygen from the water." He lifted a can of Coors Light from the table and took a sip. "Or it could have been a change in salinity—the lake might have gone from fresh to salt water."

Then, nothing from anyone. No questions, no comments, just pleasant expressions and nods around the table. Nothing more from George.

"Did you say the job was in Kemmerer, George?" asked Lorraine's brother, Uncle Frank.

"Just west about fifteen miles," George answered.

Lorraine leaned across the table and whispered to me, "You know, honey, Kemmerer, Wyoming, is the home of the very first JCPenney store in the United States of America."

I nodded. I did know that. I think that's all anyone ever knows about Kemmerer.

"Did you go the Riverton way or clear to Rawlins?" continued Uncle Frank.

"I came home through Riverton, but on the way down I had to pick up some equipment in Laramie, so I went through Rawlins."

Uncle Frank said, "Goin' through Muddy Gap, you better be sure you fill up in Casper because there's nothin' on that road."

Everyone agreed.

Kelly's husband, Jim, looked up from his plate. "So, George, d'ya go interstate the whole way down or take the cutoff at Wheatland?"

George, in the middle of a bite of steak, said, "I got off at Wheatland."

Jim was animated now. "I tell you what, I was on that road one bitter cold night and saw the worst wreck I ever saw. A young gal in a new Camaro smacked a muley. Looked to me like the muley won."

There, they found it, the sweet spot. Now they were off and running—highways, cars, wildlife, and weather. Everyone could relax, especially me.

Before we left, Lorraine took George and me aside to make sure we'd go to the Rodeo parade the next day. I often skip it, and she probably knew George might also because he'd be leaving again soon. I had noticed, too, that this was the first year in a long time Lorraine hadn't offered to take Clara to the parade. Anyway, she said she'd be in front of Olsen's Trophy Shop, she had someone she wanted us to meet and his name was Tom Baxter. I'd never seen her like that before. As far as I knew, she hadn't had a boyfriend since George Sr. died. Her eyes were alive and bluer than ever, and she truly looked like a teenager with a crush. She said she was sure I'd enjoy meeting him because he was from back east—Ohio.

chapter 3

The town where I grew up, Bristol, Massachusetts, is now essentially a suburb. Husbands go to Boston each day by car or by the commuter ferry between nearby Hingham and Rowe's Wharf. Wives and children stay in Bristol, hardly leaving and seeming to have no idea what the men do every day in their suits and stiff leather shoes.

I think the transformation from small town to suburb began during my childhood, but for me and my family, Bristol was a place unto itself. My father, a banker, came home for lunch every day, and my mother sat at the kitchen table to eat with him. They talked about what they had read in the *Boston Globe* that day and goings-on in the family. Sometimes they mentioned an event at the Boston Public Library, or a book or an upcoming exhibit at the Museum of Fine Arts. My mother was nice and sweet then, the kind of person who could give you a hug and you felt better. She was still a lot like her mother in that way.

Sunday dinners were often at my grandparents' house around the corner in their grand, white clapboard Victorian with dark green, nearly black shutters and a distant view of the Bristol harbor. We ate by candlelight at a table under a portrait of a Charles Linscott, an ancestor from way back. In addition to my grandparents, any number of relatives might be there—sometimes aunts and uncles and cousins, sometimes old great-aunts, sometimes just my parents, my younger brother, John, and me. On the nights that went beyond what must have been my bedtime, I remember most clearly my father and my grandfather. They were like an act of sorts—Dad leading and egging on with questions and Granddad happily entertaining whoever sat at the table.

There were stories of my great-grandmother's trip to Russia in the twenties—"a time when no one went to Russia," we were told; tales about my great-grandfather's cousin, a maiden lady who lived on Elm Street at the edge of Bristol with a virtual menagerie, including a caged monkey in the dining room. A daredevil who loved animals more than people, she had parachuted and even once rode a motorcycle right up onto the town selectman's front porch. But the story that sticks out most in my mind, because of a line so often quoted, was about my grandmother's father, Tommy O'Keefe, arriving in this country from Ireland. According to the story, he was such a charming, quick-witted young man, he was no more off the boat in Boston than he had two job offers. One with a shoe factory in western Massachusetts and one with a shipping company in Bristol. He couldn't decide between the jobs, so he flipped a coin—heads Bristol, tails Holyoke. Heads it was, so Bristol won him. Bristol is where he took the job and Bristol is where he stayed, where he met his wife and where they raised their daughters. At that point in the story, Granddad would switch into an Irish accent and quote old Tommy O'Keefe: "'So none of you would be here if 'tweren't for the flip of a coin …'" I can't say how many times I heard that line, "If 'tweren't for the flip of a coin …"

A late night in that house never ended without a song or two, or twenty. Granddad knew the words to more songs than you can imagine.

If my nighttime memories are of my grandparents' house, then daytime, if not at home, was with Ms. Harding. She was another maiden New England lady who seemed to like animals better than people. She lived in a shingled quarter Cape on a small farm that's now a fancy neighborhood of enormous suburban houses called Spring Acres. She had five or six flea-bitten gray Arabs and Arab crosses. They weren't fancy, just solid, old-fashioned horses that were soft and supple to ride. In exchange for helping her with barn chores I was able to ride. Sometimes she let me go off on a trail by myself and sometimes she gave me a lesson.

Ms. Harding's facial features were straight and strong and her skin wrinkled from a life in the outdoors. She spoke in a way that must have sounded cultivated, using big words I sometimes didn't understand—"Now let me see you get an *animated* walk out of him!" In her teachings she stressed the importance of a "balanced seat" above all, and she talked of the horses' character traits as if they were human friends. She also taught me much of what I know about how to take care of a sick or injured animal. I asked her questions about the horses the way my father questioned my grandfather at Sunday dinner.

All that I remember of my childhood seems so far away now, utterly distant. Thinking of it, I almost feel it may have happened to someone other than me, there's so little connecting me to it anymore. Everything began to change, and end really, at about the time I went to college. Within a span of less than three years I lost both my grandparents and my father. First Grandma Linscott, then two years later, after a brief but awful illness, my father, and then very soon after that, Granddad.

We lost one after another, and within a very short time, and my mother was left in charge. I should have been more sympathetic to her and tried to understand her predicament, but I wasn't and I didn't. In my self-absorption, all I felt was my loss and all I saw in her was a changed person. Gone was the mother who had few opinions and encouraged me in everything, replaced by a commander determined to get me a career and the "right kind" of husband from the "right kind" of family. She left my brother alone, he was her baby, but the more he wanted to take a year off between high school and college, the more determined she became to set me on her path to my success. She became a stranger to me, someone who made me lose my nerve. She even scared me and I scared myself, afraid I'd disappoint her.

By that time I was in college, at Bowdoin, "way up in Maine," as most people in Bristol said. It was only about a three-hour drive, but they acted like I was at the North Pole; Maine seemed so remote and cold to them, the kind of place you'd avoid if you had a choice. I happily majored in American Studies—literature and history—because that's where my interest was, and still is. It was a subject my father, my grandparents, and even my "old" mother would have been thrilled about. But the new mother, the drill sergeant, couldn't understand. "What are you going to do with that?" she'd ask, frustrated with my impracticality.

It was an awful time for me, filled with grief and

confusion. And to make matters worse, everyone I was in school with, particularly the women, seemed single-mindedly driven toward a career. They appeared to know what they were going to do, what company they hoped to work for, or what graduate program they'd enter the fall after graduation. My friends spent hours upon hours discussing what they hoped to get out of their careers, what they were after in life. They were probably the daughters my mother should have had. I, on the other hand, had no idea. I'd sit in the dorm rooms listening to these conversations, half panicking inside, but making sarcastic comments like, "Go ahead, guys, you do everything you can to get a career. I'm going to do everything I can to avoid one!"

As graduation approached, the big question, "What are you going to do?," was everywhere. In hindsight I realize it was just an easy question for people to ask, the way they ask a child, "How old are you?"; they think they are throwing you a big, easy underhand softball just to start a conversation, but to me it seemed like the world was waiting with bated and ever so interested breath to see what Kate Vaile would do with her life and her sensational degree in American Studies. Would she teach? Would she go to graduate school? Would she work at a library? You know how she loves to read. Maybe she'll go to law school—you know a lot of English majors go into law—but wait, what *was* her major? It wasn't English, was it?

So when I met George on the train soon after college and he brought me to Wyoming, it was as if a new type of person and then a new world were revealed to me. First, George was a man who knew what he wanted to do purely because of his interests and the work itself, not because of what his career would do for him. And he loved me, even the me without a clear direction. Second, Wyoming was a place where people hardly ever ask what you plan to do next, what your ambitions are, what you're interested in, or even much about where you've come from and what's happened to you in the past. People seem to care about the moment and politely never want to pry. What a relief it was to me!

The space, isolation really, relieved me, too. There's a hometown feeling that encompasses the entire state, yet the distances remove anything that in another place I might have interpreted as oppressive. George said he'd read a description of Wyoming once that said the whole state was really just a small town with very, very long roads. And, oh my God, what long roads! High school kids ride for seven hours on the bus just to play in a regular old basketball game. Once when we were driving a section of highway, through the Shirley Basin, George pointed out to me that we hadn't seen a house, a store, a barn, or a building of any kind for more than ninety miles. I remember he also wanted to be sure I realized that from the car windows within our view was an area about the size of the whole state of Massachusetts.

After George and I were married and I came to Hayden to live, my first job was exercising some horses and doing barn work for a rancher west of town. You might imagine how the job thrilled my mother! Anyway, I went to meet Wayne Fritz for the first time and I started right in telling him all about my experience with horses. He stood politely for a bit, and when I finally slowed down, realizing I was answering questions he wasn't asking, he handed me a pitchfork and said, "Let's see how you do with this." He pointed to a stall at the end of the barn. As I headed away from him, slightly embarrassed, he called, "Don't strip it."

When I was done with the stall he nodded and pointed to a mare on the cross ties.

"Now tack her up. You can ride in the round pen and then if that all goes well, why, you take her up on the ridge."

That was the interview, and at the end of an hour and a half, I had the job.

I thought, Wow, what a place! No questions, no show-me-how-accomplished-or-smart-you-are attitude, just can you do it? And how are you doing today?

After so many years living here, it's funny to think that those things that appealed to me so in the beginning tend to be what can annoy me most now.

chapter 4

I wanted to meet Tom Baxter, but I never expected to
like him as immediately as I did. It's not that I thought
I wouldn't like him, it's just that I assumed I wouldn't
feel one way or the other about a boyfriend of Lorraine's.
When Tom Baxter stood up to shake my hand in the
sharp sunlight in front of Olsen's Trophy Shop, I was
interested in him right away. There's a short story by
Willa Cather called "Neighbor Rosicky." Rosicky, an
immigrant and a city man, was successfully farming in
the American Midwest. His eldest son married Polly, a
good-hearted young woman who had somewhat sophis-
ticated tastes, and the son brought her to the country to
homestead. With hardly any talk, a quiet kinship and understanding, perhaps it was love, developed between old
Rosicky and Polly. It was calm and it was affectionate and
it was uncomplicated. When I first met Tom, I sensed
suddenly that I knew better than ever how young Polly
must have felt about her father-in-law, Rosicky. Maybe it

was the way he looked right at me, like he gave a damn, or maybe somehow I sensed we had something in common, or maybe it was just his hands, warm and brown, like Rosicky's.

. . .

In small towns like Hayden there's an unusual attachment to holidays and parades, and here, Rodeo is the biggest event of all. There is something for everyone—joggers can put on their cowboy boots and hats and run in the Boots & Spurs Road Race, cooks can enter two cook-offs, Biscuits & Gravy and Chile & Cinnamon Rolls, and husbands can easily find the company to stay out all night. For the parade, everyone in town turns out. Even those who grew up here return from cities and suburbs to show their children and remind themselves of what they see as the romance of small-town life in the West. Businesses close. Mr. Stanley respects the town's traditions and locks tight the doors of his office. Old people, parents, and little children patiently watch, as good as gold, and the rest start drinking early, spilling out onto sidewalks in front of the dark barrooms of The Bronco and The Proud Cut. There's no law against open containers, so on parade morning, beer sloshes around in all kinds of cups on Main Street.

Lorraine must have planted herself in the spot in front of the trophy shop very early. Her orange and green plastic lawn chairs were essentially orchestra seats, front and center. She was so close to the street that her clean white sneakers rested on the curb and she had a perfect view of the Aberdeen-Main intersection, right where the parade takes a turn. Tucked beneath her were a small cooler and a big tan purse. The parade had already started by the time we found her, and Clara was nearly out of her mind with worry that she might have missed the Rodeo Princess.

"Grammy! Grammy! Did we miss her?" she yelled when she saw the back of Lorraine's head.

"Who, sweetheart?"

"The Rodeo Princess!"

"Oh good heavens no. Honey, you know the Rodeo Princess is always last."

Tom, in a straw cowboy hat and pressed light green shirt, nimbly stood from his chair next to Lorraine as soon as he realized we had arrived. He was neat and trim, medium height, with grayish-white hair. I thought he was probably in his mid-sixties, a bit older than Lorraine. Except for a bump near the bridge, his nose was as straight as an arrow. He took off his sunglasses—the eyes were as blue as Lorraine's—tipped his hat, shook hands, and called us by our names. The handshake was firm, the kind I like. I can't stand it when a man gives me a sad little shake, like a woman can't handle the real thing. He took his time to look at each of us individually, not as if he were sizing us up, but more like he might want a lasting picture in his mind. Rushed he was not—not by the commotion, or by the excitement of the day, or by Lorraine, who literally leaped from her chair and nearly danced around each of us making the introductions.

People around us, and Clara, were intent on watching the parade, so there wasn't much time for standing chitchat. Tom offered me his seat, I refused, and he insisted, so I sat down next to Lorraine. She elbowed me and I smiled and nodded, but kept my face looking straight. I think she giggled.

Tom and George were standing behind and I realized that Tom was soon asking George a million questions about paleontology. George talked freely and was even animated. Then I was in one of those situations that drive me crazy—two conversations going on at the same time and I'm more interested in listening to the other than to the one I'm in. It's rude and I know it, but sometimes I can't help myself. Lorraine was so wrapped up in the excitement of the day, I doubt she noticed.

It was at least her fifty-fifth Rodeo parade and she had a running commentary on all that was passing before us. The governor's wife wore the same yellow dress to the inaugural ball in Cheyenne, she was certain. The Mountain Motors float was not up to standards this year. Then along came the Hayden Home Health Care nurses.

"Oh, Kate, do you see that gal right there?"

"Which one?"

"That one, right there." She leaned forward in her chair as if getting a bit closer would help me see. "The gal with the curly red hair. Right there. At the back."

"OK. Yup. I see her."

"She's the one I told you about, Dannie Rae—remember her daughter graduated with Kelly."

It didn't ring a bell, but Lorraine didn't notice.

"Well, I'm just dying to see her bedroom. Evidently, it's gorgeous—a patriotic theme. She has red carpet and blue striped wallpaper with a stencil star border. Sandy told me she got the stencils at Coast to Coast. Her pillow shams look like the American flag, and I imagine the drapes do, too. Betty, at work, says Dannie Rae even made a marvelous red, white, and blue quilt. Now, I wouldn't know if that's on the bed or hanging on the wall."

How awful it sounded, and I didn't know what to say. "Wow. I've never heard of anything like that," I fumbled. "I wish I could see it."

"So do I, honey. Soooo do I."

Meanwhile, I was trying to listen to Tom, who was asking about mineral rights and the regulations for selling bones found on state lands. George explained that anyone can take a reasonable amount of invertebrate fossils or petrified wood from BLM land (Bureau of Land

Management), but vertebrate fossils can only be removed by scientific permit, and then they must go to a public collection.

Lorraine talked with Clara, so I could listen better to what was being said behind me.

"So you can't sell them at all?" Tom asked.

"No, not if they're on public land. The laws are actually terrific for people like me who are in it for the discovery and the science as opposed to the treasure hunters."

"What about the rancher over in the Dakotas who sold the dinosaur to the museum in Chicago for ten million dollars? There was quite a controversy as I remember—government, the rancher, the museum, and the Sioux got involved, too, I think."

"Oh yeah," George answered. "That was really complicated and set the precedent."

You could have blown me over with a feather! What was this? A real conversation? Could this be someone who seemed seriously interested in something? How far this was from driving routes and my all-time favorite question, "You been busy?" I was ready to jump up and hug and kiss Tom Baxter right then and there! I wondered if George felt the same way.

The heat was staggering. I remember my sunglasses slid down my sweaty nose, and Clara was tugging at my arm.

"Mummy. Mummy. Listen to Grammy."

It must have been somewhat reluctantly that I turned my attention to Lorraine and my little girl.

"Oh, I was just telling Clara about James Conroy." Lorraine pointed across the street. "Do you see that building there? That used to be the Hotel Continental."

It was now a brown popcorn shop called Bear Creek Traders.

"See that little bitty door on the side?"

I nodded. Clara gripped my arm.

"The outlaw James Conroy came down those very steps and shot the sheriff."

"Mummy, did you hear that?" Clara didn't wait for an answer. She turned to Lorraine. "When?"

"Well, I don't know, honey. A long time ago." Lorraine's eyes were back on the passing parade and she was done with the James Conroy story, but Clara wasn't.

"Why did he shoot him?"

"I wouldn't know, honey. I guess because he was bad and the sheriff was the sheriff." Lorraine pulled a juice box and some crackers from the cooler beneath her chair and handed them to Clara.

The high school marching band came along playing a jazzed-up version of "It's a Grand Old Flag," and Lorraine and Clara clapped and bounced to the beat. A short girl with bleached blond hair and a well-rehearsed smile twirled the baton around her thick thighs. I looked behind me, and George was standing alone. He explained where Tom had gone by putting his hand up to his ear and mouthing, "Phone call."

Behind the band was the Hayden School District float. The superintendent of schools sat at a desk with his secretary, Dalene Koltiska, seated behind him. I looked at Lorraine, and her expression was suddenly stiff. She looked straight ahead, but must have felt my eyes because she shook her head no, meaning, No, nothing had changed. Dalene, the superintendent's secretary, used to be Lorraine's best friend. They grew up together, and as everyone who went to Hayden High says, they "graduated together." They were like sisters, maybe closer than sisters. They were bridesmaids in each other's wedding, they had children at the same time and now could have grandchildren in common, but that part of life they don't enjoy together. Lorraine once told me what happened. Years ago, when she and Dalene were in their forties, they played in a bowling league together. Their team, the Lucky Ladybugs, was good—champions, in fact. Apparently Lorraine was the team spirit and Dalene the talent. Anyway, after bowling the two of them would often go to a pizza place with a bar and "get snockered." One night Dalene began complaining again about not having enough money. Lorraine, who readily admits to having had way too much peach schnapps that night, was sick and tired of hearing money complaints from a woman who didn't have a job. And she let fly. "Dalene," she said, "I don't want to hear another word out of you about that until you get a job. Buzzy makes good money, and every time I've heard you complain about money since you married him, I've just wanted to slap your face. A woman has no right to complain about money if she doesn't work. And don't you tell me that taking care of your kids is working. Sure, it's work, but plenty of women do both; I'll tell you from experience, that's a heck of a lot more work. If you make the choice to be a housewife, then you give up the right to complain about money. Go get a job and then complain all you want, but until then SHUT UP!"

"*You* shut up, Lorraine Colter," Dalene shouted back.

"Not about that I won't. 'I want this, I want that, but we can't afford it … Buzzy better get a raise or start looking for another job.' Well, Dalene, I've had it with that."

"You say you've wanted to slap my face for years."

"Yup. Every time I've heard that kind of talk out of you. It's just wrong."

Then Dalene stood up, walked around the table, and slapped Lorraine's face hard. And that was it, the end of their friendship. Lorraine still visits Dalene's mother at the nursing home, and she sent Dalene a card when she heard Buzzy's diabetes had taken a turn for the worse. For her part, Dalene sent flowers to the funeral home when George Sr. died, but I don't think Lorraine will ever forget that she wasn't at the funeral. In any case, some old loyalties are still there between them, but the friendship is gone. Lorraine says they would probably still be friends if only Dalene would have it out with her, but when they run into each other, Dalene acts as if nothing happened. She smiles and talks about her kids. I'll never forget what Lorraine said to me and George about that: "I can stand a lot in people, but they have to be straight with me. I know dishonesty is the worst thing there is and, if you ask me, acting fake is just a lie of another kind."

As the school district float passed by, Dalene looked over at our group from her perch by the superintendent. She grinned brightly and waved faster when she caught Clara's eye. I didn't dare look to see if Lorraine waved at all.

By now Tom had returned from making his phone call and he leaned down, put his head between Lorraine and Clara, and whispered in Clara's ear. She stood right up and bent forward trying to see way down the street. Then she jumped up and down squealing, "You're right! Here she comes!"

Tom, who must have been paying attention to Clara

right from the beginning, said, "Everyone, get ready for the Rodeo Princess!"

When she was still fifty yards away the Rodeo Princess's belt buckle was like a hubcap shooting out blinding light whenever the sun hit it just right. She was flanked on either side by younger girls, the Junior Rodeo Princess and Little Miss Rodeo.

The Princess rode a palomino, and the two smaller girls were on shiny bays. One carried the American flag and the other the Wyoming state flag, and each took her job very seriously. The Princess carried nothing at all, freeing her right hand for waving. As always, all three wore light blue eye shadow and shiny red lipstick, and their long hair, fresh off the hot rollers and doused with Final Net, cascaded out from under 5X beaver cowboy hats. The Princess was adorned with an elaborate rhinestone tiara resting on the brim of her hat. The crowd cheered and cheered as they rode past, and Clara turned to us all and gasped, "She's so pretty."

Before I could answer, Tom said just what I wanted to say, only it was much better coming from him.

"Sure, she's beautiful, Clara. But what matters is that she's the best rider. She can ride like the wind and get around those barrels faster than anyone. Pretty's pretty, but it doesn't much matter."

We all smiled, especially George. He knew how Tom's explanation would please me.

The town picnic is held after the parade and I usually skip it because it's always the same—hot and crowded and smells like lighter fluid. The food is never anything but charred hamburgers, the perfectly round frozen kind; potato chips; and rock-hard brownies. Last year I wanted to go for one reason, and that was to find out more about Tom Baxter. Which I did.

Tom and Lorraine had met at Mountain Vision. He came in because he lost his prescription sunglasses, only he called them "dark glasses," a term I hadn't heard for years, probably not since my grandfather used to say it at the beach when I was a little girl. I guess Tom came into the eye doctor's office and Lorraine started chatting, as she always does. One thing led to another, and soon they had a plan to meet for coffee.

"One day we're having coffee," Tom said, "and the next thing I knew, she was asking me if I was going to the Bed Races!"

The Bed Races are another Rodeo event. Teams of contestants dressed in pajamas jump on all kinds of wheeled beds at the top of High School Hill and race to the bottom. As George says, if you've seen it once, you've seen it a million times.

"I forgot he was from out of town." Lorraine blushed. "I guess that might have sounded sort of weird."

"Weird's not the right word, Lorraine," Tom said with a wide smile. "I thought, My, this girl's pretty and she's forward, too."

"Well, at least she didn't ask you to Butt Darts!" laughed George.

I could tell Tom's eyes were wide, even behind his sunglasses.

George then happily explained a Hayden tradition like no other, Butt Darts. "On the last night of Rodeo, after bull riding, a well-oiled crowd gathers at the indoor round pen at the fairgrounds." He took the time to explain to Tom, "It's an old round brick building with rickety wooden bleachers around the walls and an open dirt space in the middle. It's like a theater-in-the-round for livestock.

"Competitors squeeze a quarter between their butt cheeks, then walk an obstacle course, without dropping the quarter. At the end they have to drop it right from the rear end into a cup on the floor." George stood up from the grass and pretended to put a quarter between his cheeks. He walked bent-kneed and stiff in a circle around our group. Everyone was laughing, and Lorraine just shook her head and covered her face with her hands.

George continued, "Music plays as each person—

now, you have to imagine ALL types—does the course, and whoever does every obstacle and gets the quarter in the cup wins."

"I've gotta see this!" said Tom. "Lorraine"—he took off his hat in mock chivalry—"will you go to Butt Darts with me?"

"I will NOT," she answered. "It's deesgusting! And much too late for me."

Everyone was in a grand mood and the ice cream stand was open. Tom peeled a five-dollar bill off a sizable wad of cash he pulled from his front pocket. I wondered about a thin white scar trailing across the back of his hand and up under his cuff. He handed the money to Clara and told her to go buy the biggest cone they would make her. I nodded my approval when Clara looked my way. She walked past me and whispered, "I'll get sherbet, Mummy."

The conversation moved easily from topic to topic. Tom said he wanted to see the Custer Battlefield and asked how far away it was. I felt a pang of guilt because the Battle of the Little Bighorn is really the only nationally significant historic site near Hayden and there I was, Miss American Studies, and I'd been there only once, and that was years ago. Then somehow we got on the subject of old people and Tom entertained us with stories of three old sisters he knew. I won't be able to tell it in the charming way he did, but here's the story: Three old ladies, sisters, lived together. They were old—I mean old—but that didn't hold them back one bit. They went out at night and they went on trips, driving a spiffy Packard all over the place. Didn't bother them a bit that between the three of them they had only one license. "Old ladies all look the same to the police," they'd say, so whoever was driving had the license. They always felt sorry for hitchhikers, never would pass one by. The only thing was, they wouldn't let the hitchhikers in the car. No, they could have a ride, but it had to be on the running board. Those old girls drove all the way to Florida once with a hitchhiker hanging on the outside of the car.

George and I laughed and said things like, "Can you imagine that!"

"That's great."

Lorraine smiled, but I don't think she had the picture in her head, nor did she have any idea how far away Florida is from Ohio. Then she jumped in and said, "Oh, Tom. There's Betty, from work. I want you to meet her."

Without missing a beat, he said clearly, "I don't want to meet anybody."

I think it was soon after that I started in on Tom. I know I held myself back for a while, waiting to see if George might ask Tom a few questions, particularly since Tom asked so many of him at the parade. George talked, but he didn't ask Tom anything, so I started. On the ride home, George said I sure knew how to put a damper on a good time, and maybe this time I got what I deserved for asking so much. I told him I was just showing interest, like Tom showed interest in him at the parade. George thought I seemed more nosy than interested. I was mad and told George I didn't think asking Tom where he was from, what his work was, and if he had any children was really anything too personal. "It just wasn't a Pollyanna kind of story, George," I snapped. "I know that. It's not what I expected. But, you know what, I don't think he minded talking about it. In fact, I think he was relieved to get some of that out in the open with all of us. I have a feeling your mom didn't even know a lot of that about him." George said he could guarantee Lorraine hadn't known the half of it.

What I found out, what we all found out from my questions, was this: Tom had grown up in Columbus, Ohio, and spent most of his life there, except for a brief time in the service. He had a very successful hardware store, a wife, and a son. He worked every day but Sunday for nearly forty years. Then one Tuesday evening he came home from the store and found his wife collapsed in tears on the kitchen floor. Their son, their only child, had been killed in a car accident. It wasn't long after that that his wife died, too. Her heart wasn't good to begin with, and the death of the son was just too much for her. Around the same time Home Depot was moving to Columbus, so his business was headed for a major decline, or even collapse. He got out of his hardware store while it was still worth something. In less than three years Tom had lost his family and sold his business. His whole life was gone.

When Tom was talking, seated in Lorraine's folding plastic chair, everyone sat silently listening. I suppose I kept going with the questions to show I was interested, which I was. How could anyone not be? Also, I didn't want him to feel that just because what he told us wasn't expected, or easy, I didn't want to hear it. Tom spoke slowly and quite comfortably, it seemed. He struck me as a man who had suffered unimaginable tragedy and yet never wavered, never was so shaken by the experience that he questioned who he was.

He'd always wanted to travel, he said, ever since he could remember. In fact, years ago, he got in his car alone and headed to California. "I wanted so badly to see the West I had read about since I was a boy—and California. I wanted to see the Pacific," he said almost wistfully. "I got as far as Springfield." He stopped.

"And then what?" I asked. I'm sure George was cringing with me asking another question.

"I turned around," he continued. "I'll never know what made me do it, but I just turned around and went back. Never saw a thing."

Tom took a clean white handkerchief out of his pocket and wiped his brow and around his mouth. "So." He took a deep breath and smiled. "That's why I'm here now. I'm seeing the country."

"But why Hayden?" I asked.

"Ohhh, why Hayden. Well, I had to decide whether I'd go north or south first. So I flipped a coin and the northerly route won."

"So, 'If 'tweren't for the flip of a coin …'"

Tom nodded and made a clicking sound with his tongue. I'm sure behind the dark glasses he gave me a wink.

Just then his attention shifted to the Barbershop Band on the platform at the far end of the lawn. Lorraine had closed her eyes, tipped her head to one side, and was humming the tune. Tom smiled when he noticed Lorraine and then he began softly singing, not missing a word, just like my granddad.

"Oh, I haven't heard this one in a long, long time," said Lorraine. "Who was it that sang this? Tom, do you remember?"

"'Blue Shadows on the Trail,' Vaughn Monroe, 1948,"

Tom answered, then quickly returned to his own singing.

Lorraine nodded. "That's right. I haven't thought of Vaughn Monroe in years."

I understood why George was annoyed with me for asking Tom so many questions, but I didn't care. Now it was out there. We all knew what had happened to Tom and why he had come to town. And I knew then and there that I wouldn't ask Tom another thing about his life in Ohio unless he brought it up first. It would be hard for me, because I had so many things I wanted to ask, but I knew I owed him that respect.

chapter 5

I have an aunt, Joanie. I mentioned her before; she's the one who always sees to the heart of things quickly. She's a career woman, a portfolio manager for "high-net-worth individuals," in Boston. She's only twelve years older than I am, and on the surface we have so little in common, except our past and family in Bristol. She's single, always has been, and she's totally directed in her career. I'm not directed, obviously, and most of my life is wrapped up in being a mother and a wife. I'm in Hayden, Wyoming, going to Shipton's Big R Ranch Supply store and making tacos for dinner while she clicks her high heels through grand office lobbies and meets clients for drinks at the Four Seasons. We talk on the phone all the time. In fact, she's pretty much the only person besides George and Clara whom I talk to all the time. There's really no one here whom I just visit or call on the phone to chat. For a while I kept up a bit with one or two friends from Bowdoin and a few people from Bristol, but over the years that has dwindled down to pretty much nothing beyond Christmas cards. The more you keep in touch with someone, the easier it is to keep in touch—there isn't that looming bulk of time and experience upon which you have to catch up. And, since so much of life is habit, that must be a part of it, too. Joanie and I are in each other's habits.

We talk about day-to-day things, and books, and the news, and we talk about my mother, her older sister. Of the two subjects absolutely everyone in Boston talks about, the Red Sox and the Irish fugitive James "Whitey" Bulger, we discuss only Bulger. Joanie knows I have no interest in the Sox and we both do tend to be interested in crimes and criminals. Bulger and his recent disappearance certainly has fit that bill in the past few years. O. J. Simpson and his freeway ride was a big topic for us, too. George would walk through the kitchen, hear me talking about the white Blazer or Nicole Brown and Ron Goldman, and he'd just roll his eyes and half smile. Before O. J., Joanie and I talked about Charles Stuart, the Boston fur salesman who was driving his very pregnant wife home from a birthing class when they were supposedly carjacked and abducted in the rough Mission Hill neighborhood of Boston by "a black man" who then shot the pregnant wife in the head and Charles Stuart in the stomach. The whole episode was made even more

dramatic because Chuck's desperate call to 911 was re-
corded and broadcast all over New England. The wife
died, the unborn baby survived for a few days and then
he died, too. Poor, poor Chuck was devastated and all
public sympathy was with him. Then a few months later,
he shocked everyone by jumping to his death from the
Tobin Bridge. It turned out there was no carjacker. He,
Charles Stuart, murdered his wife and their baby. He'd
planned the whole thing and even conspired with his
brother, who was waiting at the appointed intersection
in Mission Hill to catch a bag with wallets, jewelry, and
the gun after Charles himself fired the shots.

I can't say Joanie's and my interest in the underworld
arises from a concern for something greater, like justice,
nor does it come from something emotional or psycho-
logical within either one of us, like a deep-seated fear of
evil, for instance. No, Joanie and I just like to talk about
all these crimes and criminals because they make for
good, fast-moving stories.

In general, Joanie supplies the information for our
conversations, because she's in the swim, but occasionally I have something for her. There once was a philan-
dering insurance agent in Powell who plotted with his
girlfriend to kill his wife and make the death look like
a suicide. They did it, they killed the poor woman, but
their story worked for only about twenty-two hours.

The insurance agent killed himself then and there, and the girlfriend is now doing major time in Lusk for being an accessory to a murder. Another time I was riding on a plane on my way back to Hayden from Boston when I sat next to a nondescript, middle-aged furniture salesman wearing a black button-down shirt and gray polyester pants. I couldn't help myself, of course, and I asked him a few questions. Shock of all shocks, he had grown up in Holcomb, Kansas—the small town Truman Capote wrote about in his book *In Cold Blood*. My traveling companion knew the Clutters, the family that was brutally murdered. He had even spoken to young Nancy Clutter at the theater in Garden City the night before she and her family were murdered in their Holcomb farmhouse. She had white ribbons in her hair—people always remember small details like that. Anyway, that plane ride with the man from Holcomb kept Joanie and me busy on the phone for weeks.

When you get right down to it, I think what keeps me and Joanie together and connected is that neither one of us ever gives up on the other, or the other's future potential. I never stop talking to and joking with her about men and dating, even though she obviously seems to be the perpetually single type. And she never stops assuming that one day my ambition will bubble up, no longer obscured and confused by day-to-day life and my worries about Clara. My mother thinks that with no career, at least my education must make me a better mother and a more engaging dinner party guest. Oh, how my life still disappoints my poor mother! Lorraine, on the other hand, I think is embarrassed by my education. Why would I go through all that and then do nothing with it? She never says anything, but she surely understands that "keeping books" for Mr. Stanley is no brilliant career. But Joanie, the most accomplished woman I know, who intellectually and professionally seems to use every ounce of everything she has, doesn't seem to be disappointed with me, at all. Somehow she still sees potential.

chapter 6

You'd never know by looking at Clara that there's anything at all wrong with her. Nor would you suspect something was amiss by the way she acts, or speaks, or moves. But deny her nourishment for a length of time that could be as short as six hours, and there would be no mistaking that there is something severely, frighteningly wrong with this child.

Clara suffers from a condition called medium chain acyl-CoA dehydrogenase deficiency, MCADD. It's a fairly rare inherited disorder, the kind that is covered in medical textbooks by a single paragraph. Normally the human body uses glucose from the foods we eat for energy, and when the glucose runs out, say when the person hasn't eaten for a while, the body switches to breaking down stored fats into components that can also be used for energy. Clara, and others with MCADD, lack the enzyme that metabolizes fat into energy. In other words, she can only get her energy from food, and when she doesn't eat for a period of time, she literally runs out of steam, so much so that her brain doesn't have the glucose it needs to function.

She seemed to George and me to be the perfect little girl, healthy and strong. We'd had quite a time having a baby in the first place, and when Clara was born we couldn't believe she was really here and she was really ours. George would sit on the couch for hours, literally, studying her face, tracing his long fingers over her features. We were so grateful to have a baby that we each caught ourselves up short whenever the urge struck to complain about the sleepless nights and the general upheaval of our lives. I had still been doing horse work, but I stopped to be home with Clara, and for the first months, George stuck very close to Hayden. He just couldn't bear to be away from us.

I did everything I'd read I was supposed to do. I breast-fed her and when she started eating food I steamed the vegetables and fruits myself and made our own baby food. I washed her clothes in Ivory Snow and then ran them through the machine again with no soap to be sure they were totally rinsed. I sang songs and I read books and whenever she cried I went to her right away. Then, about a month after her first birthday, when among a hundred other things, she was pulling the tape out of George's cassettes, flushing the toilet over and over, and screaming at the top of her lungs when I tried to put her in her car seat, she began to drive me crazy. And, to add to the problem for both of us, she had yet to sleep through a night. She'd make it until about three-thirty or four, then I'd get up and feed her just a little bit and put her back for another two hours or so. Having not had a solid night's sleep for over a year, I'd had it.

One evening George and I decided she was just in a habit of eating in the middle of the night. So we'd try to break it by having him get up with her and try to just rock her back to sleep. We braced ourselves, knowing it might be a long night, but if we were to make it work, we'd have to stick to our plan.

Like clockwork, she woke up crying. I lay in bed and George went to her. The crying stopped for a moment, and then when Clara realized I wasn't coming she began to scream. It was torture to hear, she cried and cried, her little voice shaking as she called one of her few words, "Maaaa Maaaa." I don't know how long it went on, but it seemed endless.

Suddenly it was quiet and for a brief moment I was relieved to think she might go back to sleep. Then George started yelling for me, desperately. I ran to the room, dimly lit by a Little Bo Peep night-light, and there he was holding our baby, her back arched, body rigid, and eyes rolled back in her head. I switched the light on and could see her face was slightly blue.

"It's a seizure, Kate!" he said. There was panic in his voice. "Call nine-one-one!"

The little plump, soft body in her tiny pink-rosebud pajamas then went from tonic to jerking. Everything moved, not in a fast, rhythmic tremor, but in violent, irregular spasms.

After three days in the county hospital, test after test, and very attentive consulting physicians on the phone from Children's Hospital in Denver, she was diagnosed with MCADD. The poor little thing just couldn't go without eating, and whatever energy she had left that night, she burned up working herself into a frenzy crying for me. We now know how lucky we were. She wasn't brain damaged and she had survived the incident. Twenty-five percent don't make it through the first episode.

It took some time for George and me to adjust to the fact that we had a child with a life-threatening disorder. I think we probably went through the typical emotional phases, sadness, maybe some anger, and then we got down to business. We learned as much as we could about MCADD, we read everything we could get our hands on (and still do), and even studied a college biochemistry textbook. We'd talk late at night about how we were going to handle this and what the future would be like. We knew Clara should eventually be made aware of her situation and she'd have to be realistic, but we also wanted her to have a "normal" childhood. We didn't want her living in fear. It became very clear to us both that from then on, my job, my main purpose, was to protect Clara hour to hour from dangerous dips in her blood sugar.

Mostly what it means now is that I have to be absolutely sure she eats every couple of hours. I used to check the time constantly and even wrote down whenever she ate, but now it's a part of me. I just know, even without a clock, when it's time for food. I always carry juice boxes, crackers, and gummy bears with me wherever we go, and under the passenger seat in each vehicle is an emergency kit of those mini cereal boxes, Sprite, and a syringe to squirt the soda into her mouth and down her throat if necessary. Before bed I give her a glass of juice mixed with two teaspoons of cornstarch, which releases glucose into the system slowly. She drinks it through a straw, so I'm sure she gets most of the cornstarch first, because I can't always get her to finish the juice. Somewhere around two in the morning I wake her and give her another glass of juice or, if she's resistant, which she sometimes is, then chocolate skim milk. George offers to do the nighttime duty, but I wake up automatically anyway and there hasn't been a night yet when I haven't enjoyed the relief I feel to see Clara's relaxed body breathing in her bed.

At first, I have to admit, it was overwhelming to me, but now, as long as things are going well, it's simply a matter of habit. Her condition can be managed. I do get nervous in very remote places, like out on some of George's digs, or up in the mountains. What if the car broke down and I didn't have enough food or drink for her? Too many hours of that and she could be dead. I have nightmares about being in a snowstorm and finding ourselves like Old Mother Hubbard with bare cupboards. Subconsciously it's made me not want to travel much. We didn't anyway because of the expense, but now I have very little interest. But the big worry, and a very reasonable one, is the fear of her catching a virus. A few hours of diarrhea or vomiting, and she needs to be in the hospital with an IV. So far, that's happened only once, and that was four years ago. I do worry about crowds and other kids and their bugs, so I know I tend to keep her home more than other mothers do.

In some ways, I suppose the responsibility for me as a mother is more than I bargained for. But why spend a second thinking about that? I would never in a million years wish this on someone else or on some other family to spare us. And certainly it could be exponentially worse. The only thing I do wish occasionally is that the condition was mine instead of Clara's. I'd much rather I was the one in danger.

chapter 7

When I first moved to Hayden with George, everyone—
back in Massachusetts and in Wyoming—everyone asked
me, "Are you ready for the winters?" What they should
have asked was "Are you ready for the summers?" because to me there's no question, summer, not winter, is
the killer, and July the hardest month of all. Day after
day after day of razor-sharp light and heat that doesn't
let up until well into the evening. Perspiration dries on
your skin almost immediately, and my lips are always so
chapped, I'd rather be caught without my wallet than
without ChapStick.

On the second night of Rodeo, George and I made plans
to meet his old high school friends Robbie and Janna
Jones in the grandstands at the fairgrounds. Our eighteen-year-old neighbor, Casey Williamson, who lives
just about a half mile down Bear Creek, babysat. She's
our nearest neighbor and really the only person I trust

to leave Clara with besides Lorraine. Casey is from one of the smaller Apostolic Lutheran families in the area; she's one of eight. A whole group of Apostolics moved to Hayden a few years ago from Sturgis, South Dakota, when Sturgis became overrun by the annual rally of hundreds of thousands of Harley-Davidson riders. At first people in Hayden didn't like such a crowd moving to town together. Townspeople worried about the little green metal building, the Apostolic church, that the congregation put up next to the go-cart track, and they worried that these enormous families would take over the schools. But with coal bed methane there has been a relief of economic pressure that calms fears overall, and since nothing much has changed since the Apostolics started calling Hayden home, everyone seems to have let up. Anyway, Clara loves to have Casey babysit. Casey reminds me of the older sisters you read about in pioneer families, more like a young mother than a teenager. She knows how to cook, and how to braid Clara's long hair, and she would never leave a load of laundry in the dryer if she knew it was there to be folded.

On the way to the fairgrounds to meet Robbie and Janna, George and I rode along in his truck drinking Budweiser and listening to the country-Western station, just to get in the Rodeo mood. The lyrics of each song were so simple that by the second refrain we were singing right along. I can't remember what the songs were now, but we sang loudly, smiling and laughing and taking long draws on the beer. I even slid over right next to George and sat in the middle of the bench seat with my hand on his thigh.

"Darlin', this would be perfect, if only I had my gun rack behind your lovely head," George joked.

He'd be leaving soon, back to Kemmerer, but I made myself enjoy the moment without the dread.

According to the huge red-lighted sign in front of the Hayden National Bank drive-up, the temperature was ninety-two degrees. For some reason I can't keep myself from commenting and complaining about the heat, and ninety-two seemed particularly hot for the hour. I wanted to be accurate in my complaint, but I didn't have my watch on to verify the time, so for once I decided not to mention it.

We had fun at the Rodeo that July evening, betting a dollar each on every round. The Hayden County Rodeo is one of the very few single-round rodeos left in the country. Local kids who happen to have a great ride can beat the best rodeo riders in the country. Riders come from all over the West to compete—guys with names like Cody Browne and Ty Tillard. The enormous concrete rodeo stands are so packed all three nights that once you find a seat, it's too awkward to get up and move around.

Robbie and Janna are easy to be with because they're both chatty and funny. We really don't have much in common except for George having been in school with both of them and the simple fact that we all like one another without question. Janna has long painted nails and pressed, bright-colored clothes. She loves talking about her younger sister, who was once Miss Wyoming and is now a pageant coach and interstate judge. Robbie, who had hardly been out of Hayden except for high school swim meets, went to MIT on a full scholarship. He stuck it out in Boston for the four years of college and then got himself west as fast as he could after graduation. They're thrilled to be back in Hayden now; thanks to coal bed methane, Robbie has a job running interference between ranch owners and a drilling operation.

We stood for the Rodeo Princess's flag-carrying gallop and the singing of the National Anthem. Earthy smells of horses, cows, and hay mixed with the heavy scent of fried food that hovers over the carnival behind the stands. The wind was warm by then, not hot, and the sun, nearing the top of the mountains, no longer had the bite of the day. Rising up behind the stock pens, soft green foothills led to the deep blue shadowed mountains, and the limitless sky beyond. I felt a huge wave of patriotism standing with all those people, with their hands and cowboy hats over their hearts, singing the same song we all sing, and have sung for nearly two hundred years, all over this whole country. The scene before me was pure American and pure West and I loved it all. I wished Clara were with us so I could squeeze her hand. I hoped she ate a good dinner.

Robbie, feeling proud, too, nodded his head and said, "Like a rock."

Janna must have known I didn't quite understand what he meant because she leaned over and whispered, "Chevy trucks," then her voice changed to more a sing-song tone, "'Like a rock.' You know—the Chevy commercial." Apparently, reality is a reminder of TV, instead of the other way around.

At any kind of event I watch people as much as any-thing else. As I scanned the crowd that night, a profile two full sections over and several rows above us caught my eye. It was Tom Baxter. At first I wasn't certain it was Tom because he wore a baseball hat with some kind of logo on it, the kind with a flat and high front, and dif-ferent sunglasses. He didn't seem to be talking with the people on either side of him, so he must have been at the rodeo all by himself. I waved, and even stood up and waved again, but he didn't see me. I watched him for a while. He pulled something from his pocket, looked down at it, and quickly put it away. Then he lowered his head, closed his eyes tight, and subtly made the sign of the cross. I looked away, back to barrel racing in the arena below. Somehow, even from my distance and in a very public place, it was uncomfortable for me to see Tom in such a private moment. Missing was his open expression from the day before; his face was constricted now. My eyes and my interest were an invasion, I knew. Still, I couldn't help myself. When I looked again, he was gone.

chapter 8

The phone rang early the next morning. It was Lorraine.

"Morning, honey. 'S George there? I just want to say good-bye before he leaves."

"Hi, Lorraine. He'll be glad you called. How are you?"

"I got all my watering done by seven this morning and I'm almost done with the wash for the week! I'll wait till tonight, when it cools off, to do my ironing."

"You've been busy!" I said.

"And I didn't even mention I finished my cross-stitch for Marlena Adams's new baby. It's precious—of a baby just a-smilin', with blue eyes, and I've stitched 'Peek-a-boo' acrost the top."

"Marlena Adams? Marlena Adams, the woman on television?" I asked.

"Yes. Didn't you know she was having a baby?"

"No. I guess I didn't."

"They've been talking about it on the show for months. She's having a little girl and her name is Jordan. Isn't that darling?" Lorraine didn't wait for me to answer. "It'll be her third, you know. I'll mail the gift priority tomorrow. Marlena goes on maternity leave here pretty quick, so I want to be sure it gets there before she leaves." She paused. "I wouldn't know her home address, of course."

"No. I bet that would be hard to get," I said. "Will you send it to the NBC studios in New York?" A strange picture of a blue-eyed, cross-stitch baby standing at Rockefeller Center crossed my mind. I didn't hear Lorraine's answer.

"We sure enjoyed meeting Tom the other day," I said.

"Isn't he marvelous? He loved meeting you three, too."

"We went to the rodeo last night ... did you?" I wondered if she knew Tom had been there.

"Oh no, honey. I can't stand watching that. It's pretty boring," she said.

God love her, I thought. She knows what she likes and what she doesn't, wouldn't miss the parade but the rodeo is boring!

"Tom went, though," she said. "He just wanted to see it. You know, being from back east and all, it was something he wanted to see."

"I thought I saw him, but he didn't see me. You know how crowded it gets," I said.

"I s'pose you know what happened afterward, then." Her voice was serious, but calm.

"What?" My portable phone started beeping because the battery was low.

"They found a young gal dead behind the barns. Evidently someone stabbed her."

"What? Murdered?" I couldn't believe it. "You have to be kidding?" I said, but I knew Lorraine would never joke about a thing like that. "Oh my God! Who is she—*was* she?"

"No, I am not kidding, honey. I don't know a thing about it, except for that. She wasn't from Hayden, though. I heard it on the radio this morning. They haven't arrested anybody."

I was shocked. That beautiful evening and then a murder—a murder in Hayden. There hadn't been a murder in Hayden since I'd lived here.

"Well, honey. Guess I better talk to George." Lorraine was unflappable.

I called to George and told him to take the call upstairs because the kitchen phone, the portable one, was dying.

I'd have to find out more about the murder. I felt guilty for thinking the thought, but I couldn't help it—I couldn't wait to tell Joanie all about it.

* * *

The hours before Lorraine's call that morning had been wonderful and peaceful. When I came downstairs to get my coffee I saw Clara's nest collection, arranged smallest to biggest, on the dining room table. Twigs, mud, and bits of straw had fallen onto the old rug below. Her feathers, wild turkey to tiny meadowlark, were carefully placed nearby. A heap of CDs lay on the living room floor, fallout from George's early morning search for a certain piece. He's particular about the music in his truck and usually changes the selection before a long trip. The kitchen counter, covered with mail and catalogs, for some reason didn't bother me at all that particular morning. The house seemed cheerful, and the cool of the evening was still in the air. I remember thinking I'd rather have life over organization any day. I don't always feel that way. Sometimes I crave clean and generic living, like a Holiday Inn, with Rubbermaid bins, Tupperware containers, and Lysol. But most of the time I do prefer our confusion.

George brought cereal and juice upstairs for Clara as he read to her in her bed. I've always admired the way he reads to her, taking his time like there's not another thing in the world he's worried about doing. I, on the other hand, race through stories with her, even skipping sections until she learned to read and I got caught.

When George was done talking with Lorraine, he came downstairs, hugged me, and we indicated to each other that we'd have to hold our talk about the murder until later. He whispered that he wanted to get another coat of varnish on Clara's desk, so he needed me to keep Clara from following him to the basement. She and I went out to feed the horses and finish getting the laundry off the line. The dryer was broken again.

Clara, still in the hot pink Barbie nightie Lorraine had given her, pulled on her worn cowboy boots on our way out. She'll never really know the feeling of cool grass under her feet, at least not in her own yard. Dry, clumpy grass sometimes punctuated with sneaky thistle surrounds our house.

When we got to the clothesline behind the house, Clara said, "Mummy, did Casey tell you what we saw last night?"

"She said you left the laundry on the line because you saw coyotes!" I opened my eyes wide.

"Yup. We saw three of 'em right up there." She pointed to a barren hillside covered in sagebrush behind the barn. Her hands were little and plump still.

"Wow. What did you think?" I asked.

"Mummy, I've seen 'em before!" she said. "They're cute. Casey was scared, though, so we went inside."

"Oh, I see." I pulled George's last shirt off the line, haphazardly folded it, and put it in the basket. Percy, our Border collie, lay at my feet, as usual, staring straight at me.

Clara wanted to get to the barn quickly so we could finish the chores and she could ride our old quarter horse, Sunny. I wondered if she appreciated having horses right out her back door, because hardly a day goes by when I'm not at least a tiny bit grateful for our barn and our comfortable little place. I fished a T-shirt and jeans out of the laundry basket, and she dressed in the warm sunlight behind the house. Her arms and face were tan, her shins a shade lighter, and the rest of her body pale white. I was proud of my little "Western gal," unfazed by coyotes or talk of rattlesnakes, and I was a little sad, too, looking at her small body that wouldn't really know summers on the beach. Sure, she might visit occasionally, but the feeling of dried salt on her skin would be a novelty, always slightly strange to her.

That night when I was tucking Clara into bed she said, "Mummy, you want to know something funny?" She slurped the last bit of cran-apple juice and cornstarch through the straw.

"Sure." I pushed her wispy brown hair aside and kissed her little forehead.

"I don't really want the coyotes to be on our hill, but I want to look at them again. I want to see them, but I don't want them to be there. Isn't that weird?"

I think my response was useless and bland, something like, "I know, honey. I feel like that, too, sometimes."

But what she was saying, I realize now, is bigger. That's how we all feel—it's our nature. We don't like the bad, we don't want it to be there, yet we're forever fascinated. Only the rare soul can look away.

chapter 9

At first, my aunt Joanie wasn't as interested in the Hayden murder as I thought she would be. But, in hindsight, I see I didn't have enough information to hold her attention. All I knew at that point was what Lorraine had told me on the phone. Not much, but certainly enough to get my mind racing. In Boston murders happen all the time, so a simple fatal stabbing with no story didn't have that much appeal. I forget Joanie's been in Boston so long, she's forgotten what it's like to live in a small town.

As I remember, my conversation with Joanie moved quickly from the murder to the dating service date she had been on the night before.

"Why do I keep subjecting myself to these things? Why, Kate, why?!"

"You're asking me?" I said. "I can't believe you have the strength."

"He's a broker and pretty good-looking, so I had hope at first, but the conversation—Jesus Christ—it was pathetic! A new Filofax that's changed his life and the frequent flyer miles he earns on his fabulous new credit card."

"Oh, terrific," I said. "Tell me more." Sarcasm is alive and well with Joanie and me.

"He bought his car three years ago and thought it would get twenty-five miles to the gallon, but quickly discovered it only gets twenty-three, so now he's thinking of trading it in." She went on as if this were all so interesting. "A new car every three years is probably a good idea anyway when you factor in warranties—"

"Stop!" I interrupted. "My pulse is slowing…. My eyes are rolling back…. Stop…."

"Don't you want to hear about his sensational long-distance calling plan?" she asked.

"No…. Help me slit my wrists instead…."

"I know! It was deadly. So bad that when it came to my favorite moment at the end of the date, when he says, 'I'll call you …,' I just cut him off and said, 'You know what, forget it. This isn't going to work out.'"

"You said it like *that*?"

"Yeah. I couldn't take it. I mean you just have to accept right off the bat that these people are desperate in the first place to go to a dating service. Obviously! We all know I'm desperate, too, but, Christ, I can't waste my time being *nice*. Nice is so overrated and what do I care?" Joanie took a deep breath and changed her tone. "Anyway, I have a new idea." I couldn't wait to hear what this would be.

"I just have to let Whitey know about me somehow."

She was, of course, talking again about the infamous, legendary Boston gangster, Whitey Bulger. The papers cover his story without letup and the whole state of Massachusetts knows much more about him than they do about the governor. He's on the lam—wanted by the IRS, the Boston Police Department, the Massachusetts State Police, and the FBI for everything from tax evasion to murder.

"Perfect!" I laughed. "You want him to know you're available?"

"I sure do. It came to me last night I *am* his type: blond, buxom, and don't ever forget, I'm in finance—good with numbers."

I must have been laughing out loud by then.

"His FBI poster says he likes libraries and historical sites. I could become interested in history. How hard could that be? Just read a few books and study up on it. Plus, I have no family, no real connections, so to speak, so I'm seriously available. I'd even polish his coin collection and that little pearl-handled knife."

"This is a great plan!" I said. "But doesn't he have that girlfriend with him already? The one from Quincy."

"Oh, oh, oh," Joanie spoke quickly. "For a moment I forgot you're way out there!" Then, mocking my mother, who after eleven years of me living out west still calls me and says, "What time is it out there?" Joanie continued, "Guess what, Whitey's gal pal is back in Quincy."

"Really?" I said.

"Life on the run wasn't all it was cracked up to be and she wanted to go home. Supposedly Whitey dropped her off himself last winter! Can you believe he'd have the balls to come back to Boston." It was more of a statement than a question. "What a guy! I think I'm in love already." She was on a roll.

"Yeah. What do you care if he's blown people's heads off and deals drugs? I mean in the big scheme of things, does that *really* matter? Certainly could make for better conversation than Filofaxes and frequent flyer miles!"

Joanie took a sip of something, probably coffee. She practically lives on it. I pictured her in her air-conditioned office high above Boston Harbor looking out over the cool blue water speckled with boats in the distance. From her desk she could see the rooftops of Whitey's South Boston stomping grounds and, beyond that, the girlfriend's hometown, Quincy.

She went on. "It's just too bad he didn't know about me. I could have gotten in the car minutes after the old girlfriend got out."

"He might have been too heartbroken to take you right away. Don't you think?"

"No way. He was over her a long time ago. Plus, you know they say he can*not* be without a woman. A real man's man always needs a lady's touch."

"Oh, I forgot about that."

"Seriously, I'm the right age for him. He's probably about ten years older than I am—he's in his sixties, right?—and he doesn't go for the young bimbos. He likes a mature woman."

"Yes," I said. "And don't forget what Shakespeare said, 'The prince of darkness is a gentleman.'"

"Oooooh, yes. He'll like literary references. Maybe you could tutor me in history, too."

"We could work something out," I joked.

"I just know I'm on to something here," she said.

I laughed most of the time, but Joanie feigned seriousness throughout.

I can't remember just how the conversation ended, but I do know I hung up and the phone rang a few minutes later.

"Just one more thing," she said. "I need a good picture of myself and I know who should take it!" She was excited. "I want a Sotheby's photographer."

"You do?"

"They have all those pictures of chairs and highboys

in the auction catalogs and they look fabulous, but if you see the real thing it's usually junk. Pieces of crap made to look beautiful, priceless. That's what I need. It'll be gorgeous!"

"No you don't!" I said. "Then he might be disappointed when he meets the real you."

Joanie is able to talk like this because she is attractive and she knows it. She's a big woman, not fat, but definitely big. My mother says she's "horsey," but I think she's great-looking and so does George. Why she hasn't married I don't know. It might seriously be a case of not having met the right person.

"Oh, you're right." She paused. Her voice lowered. "I didn't think that through well enough." Then she was optimistic again. "Well, I'm going to have the picture taken anyway. Use it for my obituary."

chapter 10

Frantic is always the way it feels when George is leaving for a dig. He's packing, distracted and excited, and always, without warning, he has something he needs me to do right away. There must be something wrong with me that I haven't learned to plan for his requests by freeing myself up ahead of time so as to be available on departure day, D-Day, as we call it. Or maybe subconsciously I go the other direction, busying myself, so his requests can justifiably annoy me. After so many years I seem unable to keep myself from being frustrated with him for leaving. I know it's his work, I know it's his love, I know it's how he makes the money for us to live, but still it bothers me a bit to see him leave. Also, I know Clara and I could go with him, but it makes me nervous, and I've done that enough to know that entertaining myself and Clara all day in and around Kemmerer, only to see George for dinner at Taco Time or Arctic Circle, then to sleep in an overly disinfected cinder-block cell at the Antler Motel, is not for me. Even when I feel less than charitable about George leaving, I do try to remember that each night he's away he has to lie his body down alone in those thin polyester sheets at the Antler while listening to the hum of a clunky air-conditioning unit.

Last July on the D-Day in question, I was out in the barn with Timmy, the pony with the cut pastern, on the cross ties. He was getting better, I thought, but it was slow going. If his owners, the Nicholsons, didn't seem so willing and able to invest in the recovery, I might have wondered if everyone should have been put through this for a potentially lame horse in the end. The vet they use, young and forever willing to treat at whatever cost, thought he had a good chance of a full recovery. I was more skeptical and worried that the vet was just a little too enamored with his new degree and expensive equipment. But I'm really in the service industry and I was just as happy to take care of the pony if that's what they wanted.

I'd pulled off the bandage, as I did every morning, and was ten minutes into a twenty-minute hot-water-and-Epsom-salt soak, when George came running into the barn. He tripped on the hose and caught himself, but the metal surveyor's box he carried went clattering down on the cement floor. Timmy spooked, knocking over the soak bucket.

"C'mon, George! Even Clara doesn't do that! Since when do you run in here?" I wasn't exactly yelling.

"Sorry!" he said, but it wasn't an apology. "Why can't you lighten up?"

"I was almost done and now I have to start all over!"

Here was the critical moment. His response would determine which direction it would go, a fight or a passing snap. I was ready to fight and he knew it.

"I'm *really* sorry. That was stupid," he said quietly. "I was coming in here to ask you a huge favor, but let me get you some more hot water first."

I took a deep breath and handed him the bucket.

When he returned from the house with the hot water, he kissed my cheek and said, "Would you believe I need you to help me?"

"What a shock," I said sarcastically.

"Could you, would you, please, please, please run into town for me?"

"What do you need?" I was trying to be as nice as possible.

"I just have so much to pull together to get out of here by noon that I don't think I have time to go myself."

"Another shocker," I said. "You didn't answer my question. What do you need?"

He spoke as fast as he could. "Two packs of triple A batteries, cotton rope, paper towels, Handi Wipes, a ream of paper, mechanical pencils, dental floss, razors, tube socks, ChapStick—"

"George!" I was exasperated, but couldn't help thinking it was funny, too. So typical. "What is wrong with you?"

"I know, I know, I just forgot...."

"You are unbelievable. Forget the razors and dental floss—they're under the sink in the bathroom—and you better write the rest down for me."

He pulled a list from his back pocket, written out in clear capital letters.

"This means Wal-Mart," I said.

"Wal-Mart." He knew how much I hated going there, but there really was no choice sometimes.

I resoaked Timmy's leg, squirted a syringe of salt water under the ragged edge of the cut for a final flush, dried it all off, coated the wound with gooey yellow Fura-Ointment, covered it with gauze, and wrapped the pastern with fresh white cotton and fluorescent pink vet wrap. Clara loves the pink. Then I rushed through the rest of the barn chores, worrying I'd forget to do something important.

Clara, who was walking Percy all around the yard between the barn and house on a leash, had no interest in going with me to Wal-Mart once she heard there wouldn't even be time to look at the Barbies, let alone get one. She was pretending Percy was in a dog show; he'd already won the Border Collie Class and Working Dogs and, as Clara explained to me, they had a "long way to go to be ready for Best in Show."

Fast is how I normally drive, so the trip to town that day wasn't unusual. I didn't know exactly what time it was because my truck doesn't have a clock and I couldn't find my watch, but I did know there wasn't time to waste. I decided I would, however, take three extra minutes to buy a Barbie to put aside for Clara's birthday.

If the Hayden Wal-Mart's open, the parking lot is jam-packed, no matter when you go. People idle in their cars waiting for parking spaces to open up near the door. They must not think about the miles walked once inside; maybe it's the sheer quantity of stuff there for the buying that distracts people from even realizing they are walking in the store. The waiting for a nearby parking space is as if physical movement in the sun and air were the only kind to be avoided.

With George's list in hand, I took a deep breath before getting out of the truck, and I did what I always do before I walk beneath the big, bright white star dividing the words "Wal" and "Mart"—I said to myself, "You can do it. It's not that bad. Just don't look for a window, don't wish for someone to help you, and don't even think about the lighting. Go in. Don't get frustrated. Don't be depressed. You can do it."

Once inside, I remembered I should have brought a sweatshirt. The air-conditioning is always cranked up and the place was freezing. I also should have kept my eyes glazed over. Unfortunately I didn't, and there before me was a quickly dwindling pile of white, red, and black boxes. Singer sewing machines—on sale. Shoot. Why did I notice that? I thought. I promised Lorraine that if I ever saw sewing machines on sale I would call her right away, and now here they were and I was in a rush. For an instant I considered pretending I hadn't seen them, but I couldn't. I promised, and a promise *is* a promise.

I waited at customer service for a mouse-toothed woman to get her manager's permission to let me use the phone.

Lorraine was ecstatic.

"Oh, sweetie, that's marvelous! I'll be right down. I can't believe I didn't know about this! Oh, you know how I've been waiting for a new machine! Tom's here with me, we were on our way out to pick chokecherries, but we'll come down there right now." I didn't have a chance to get a word in. "You are the sweetest daughter-in-law anyone ever had. Do me a favor, honey. Wait by those machines and save me one. We're on our way!"

She hung up. Damn it. Now I had to stand there waiting for her, wasting precious time.

By the time I got back to the machines, the stack was smaller, so I knew I couldn't risk it now. I took deep breaths, rocked up and down on my heels, closed my eyes, tipped my head back, and then in came Lorraine's friend, well, I guess you'd call her ex-friend, Dalene. She had on a light pink T-shirt and shorts made of the same plaid as a small border on a T-shirt pocket. She was scented, like a candle or the fuzzy lavender powder puff I had as a little girl.

We said hello and she stopped, asked for George and Clara, told me about each of her kids, and, of course, she mentioned the murder.

"I heard it was a young gal from Colstrip, down here for the summer waitressing at the Bar 21," Dalene said. "Don't know anyone who knew her. You know how those ranch kids out there keep to themselves."

Then she asked my favorite question: "You been busy?"

I wanted to say, No. Never been busy in my life, but I answered politely, "Oh yes, trying to help George get off on a dig. Now I'm waiting here for Lorraine."

Dalene's perky expression never changed, but she quickly said, "Well, I better get to my shopping."

Whenever I see Dalene I can't help but think of her fight with Lorraine, and I'm usually reminded that I should always be more grateful to George for all he does.

I wondered if Dalene and Lorraine would run into each other in the craft aisle, by the Styrofoam Christmas tree forms and fabric paints. Just then Lorraine came rushing through the doors, turning her head this way and that, eyes darting about as a hunter's might in the forest, feet moving in short, light strides. Through the open sliding doors, I could see, out in the bright parking lot, Tom calmly helping an old woman load blue plastic shopping bags into her trunk.

"Oh, honey, thank you!" Lorraine exclaimed. Then she came right up next to me, her mouth near my ear. She spoke quickly and quietly.

"Not a word about the murder in front of Tom. Evidently he doesn't like to talk about it *at all*. He just doesn't like violence one little bit." She stepped back. "Well, neither do I, of course, but you know what I mean."

I nodded and my mother-in-law turned to the sewing machines. "Marvelous! This is just what I want. See, honey, it has the one-step buttonholer, eighteen stitch patterns, and let me see ... does it have the ... Oh yes it does! The top-drop bobbin!"

Tom walked up from behind Lorraine. He had a genuine smile for me, and even a kiss on the cheek. I was struck not only by how neat he was—pressed shirt, buttons perfectly aligned with his belt buckle—but also by how physically fit he appeared to be. He wasn't a big man, but his shoulders were broad, hips narrow, and stomach flat. He looked like an aged athlete who hadn't given up on his physique.

"Boy, are you the hero today, Kate," he said.

"No I'm not. I promised."

"And a promise is a promise," he said. Then turning to Lorraine: "This gal is something." He put his hand on her shoulder. "I've learned more than I ever knew there was to know about roses and petunias in the last few days. She knows how to *do* things and *make* things. If I were on a sinkin' ship I sure hope I'd get in her lifeboat! This gal's a survivor."

Lorraine beamed as he squeezed her shoulder. "Now she's taking me out to get chokecherries. We're making chokecherry jelly!"

You can pick chokecherries all up and down the county roads in the summer. They're awful to eat, but loaded with sugar and pectin, the jelly isn't so bad.

"Lorraine makes the best chokecherry jelly there is," I said.

"Isn't George leaving today?" Tom asked.

"Yeeeessssss," said Lorraine, "and sure as sugar, Kate's here gettin' him stuff for his trip. He's an absentminded son of a gun!"

I nodded and Tom said, "I can't wait to hear what he finds. Sounds to me like this dig could be big."

"Oh, he's always up to something," Lorraine answered before I could respond.

"Must be hard on you, Kate, being without George," said Tom. "Bet you wonder what the heck you're doing way out here when he's not home."

My eyes felt like they would well up with tears. That's exactly what I think EVERY time he leaves, and I was sure it had never occurred to another living soul.

"On the bright side," he continued, "bet it gives you more time to read." He still had his sunglasses on, but clearly he was staring straight at me.

How did he know?

Just as I said, "That *is* the bright side," Lorraine jumped in. "Well, honey, Tom and I better get going. Those chokecherries aren't going to pick themselves!"

Tom hoisted a sewing machine from the floor and they headed off to the checkout line.

When I got home George's truck was pulled up to the back door. Everything looked in order—Dvořák's *New World Symphony* and the *Journal of Paleontology* on the passenger seat, a bottle of water in the drink holder, sunglasses on the dash, and his ancient duffel bag filling the passenger side floor. I checked the little zippered pocket on the side of the duffel bag and it was still there—an old wrinkled picture of me holding Clara when she was eight months old. The back of George's truck looks like a traveling lab. He had a custom case made with flip-up doors along the side in addition to the usual rear entry. There's a place for everything: pry bars, shovels, soft-bristled paintbrushes, two computers and global positioning system (GPS) equipment, sample bags, and a traveling specimen cabinet. Sometimes I think he might be as excited about the equipment as he is about fossils and bones.

Clara, still outside behind the house, was halfheartedly swaying on the swing George made for her. She ran right to me, yelling, "Can I look in the bags?" For once I was fully prepared, the birthday Barbie well hidden under the seat next to the emergency food kit.

Surprised, and a bit annoyed, I heard the obnoxious buzz of George's tools, possibly the chop saw, coming from the basement. He was nearly done with Clara's desk, and why exactly I had to make the trip to Wal-Mart when apparently he had time to do woodworking, I didn't quite understand. But I wouldn't say a word, or even ask a question, because an unpleasant departure is unpleasant indeed. And maybe, just maybe, he was down there fixing the screen door that had been torn all summer or maybe he was making a threshold for the living room doorway.

* * *

Not at all surprisingly, George hadn't been fixing the screen door, nor had he made the threshold, but he thanked me genuinely for my help, and his good-bye kiss showed unmistakably how he'd miss me. As his arm waved out the driver's side window from under the two big cottonwoods at the end of our driveway, I had my usual sinking feeling knowing Clara and I would be alone for nearly three weeks. George would return having managed an entire team on an important dig. He had a chance to make a mark this time.

Time for me in Hayden without George is an ineffable mix of duty and emptiness. Even with my most treasured little companion, Clara, at my side, I still have the sense that if George isn't with me, I'm just waiting it out. I guess that's all life really is anyway, the passing of time. But with George, I'm always surrounded by his kindness and his unwavering interest in the world beneath our feet, and he gives me a feeling that there has to be so much more.

chapter 11

The mystery of the Hayden Rodeo murder was solved quickly. Dalene was right; the victim was an eighteen-year-old girl, Amber Perkins, just out of high school in Colstrip, Montana. She came down to work as a waitress at one of the dude ranches, the Bar 21. In the picture in the *Hayden Press* she looked pretty, with a round full face and smooth skin, and except for something about the eyes, she looked older than her eighteen years. I thought of Kelly, George's sister, always put together, hair fixed, and plenty of new clothes from strip malls in Rapid City. Before graduation last spring, it came to light in Colstrip that Amber and the new social studies teacher had secretly taken up with each other. Perhaps her parents sent her to work at the Bar 21 just to give her some time away from the gossip mill of Colstrip. The social studies teacher was fired by the school district at the end of the year, but he stayed close enough to keep an obsessive eye on his young friend. She went to the rodeo the night George and I were in the stands—the night I saw Tom there alone—with a new beau, a wrangler from the Bar 21. Amber and the wrangler went to the stock sheds after the bull riding to see some of his friends who had been competing and to have a few beers in the dim light. Into the group, out of the blue it seemed, stepped a clean-cut man wanting to talk to Amber. It appeared she was pleased to see him, and she excused herself from the group to talk with him alone.

That was the last time anyone saw Amber Perkins alive. It couldn't have been very long before her heart quit beating forever on dusty ground between two gooseneck horse trailers.

Police found the social studies teacher the next afternoon, asleep in his Toyota Camry at Sand Turn lookout in the mountains. Amber's blood was on his clothes and under his fingernails.

It was the morning after George left; I had forty-five minutes or so before I needed to wake Clara up for something to eat. Leaning over the paper on my kitchen counter, I read the story of the murder. My mind raced, conjuring up image after image, and one question after another. I pictured the officer standing on the front deck of Amber's parents' house in windswept Colstrip, delivering the grim news. I imagined the mother of the social studies teacher somewhere in the Midwest wondering what it could have been that she did wrong. How could her son have turned out like this? Who knew he had the capability for such horror? I thought of the poor wrangler, probably a nice and simple boy with a crush, wondering why he had let such a pretty girl out of his sight. He probably didn't like her stepping into the darkness with the other man, but in his gentleness he wouldn't have wanted Amber to think he was too forward, too much too soon, either. And last of all, I thought of Amber. Was she happy at first to see the social studies teacher? Maybe she was thrilled he had come for her at last. They would be together again. Or was there fear, even just an element, a tightening in the throat or a dampness of the palms? Did she see the knife coming? When did she understand that this was how she was to die? Could she see the look on his face, or was it too dark? Did the blood feel hot as it flooded past her waistband, into her pants, and then down her legs? Whom did she think of before the life left her—her parents, her best friend, or something else like a teddy bear or an angel? Where was her body now, back in Colstrip, paled to gray with the young flesh sinking against the bones?

The phone rang, snapping me out of my interior world. It was Lorraine. "Honey, did you get the paper?"

"I did. Isn't it awful?"

"Well, it sure is. It's just pitiful. That poor, poor girl. Hard to believe it happened right here in Hayden." In the next breath she asked, "Did George get off?"

"He did, yesterday afternoon."

"Tom's going up to Custer one of these days," she said.

"When's he going?" I asked.

"Oh, I don't know, honey, but I'm sure not taking a day off for that. Well … I've got my new sewing machine all set up. Don't tell Clara, but I'm going to make her a sleeping bag for her birthday. Coast to Coast has the most darling teddy bear Polarfleece."

"Oh, she'll love it."

"Of course, I've had an outfit for her for months, but this will be just a little something extra from Grammy."

"That's so nice of you."

"I sure hope my cross-stitch makes it to New York in time. They toured the nursery at Marlena's house on the show this morning because she's just about to start her maternity leave. Oh my Lord, it was gorgeous! 'Course, Marlena lives in a mansion."

"I'd imagine she would," I said.

"Can I bring anything for the party?" Lorraine was back to Clara's birthday again.

"To Clara's birthday party? Oh gosh, I don't know." The birthday was still three weeks away, and planning ahead has never been my forte. "You know what … no. Don't bring anything. You're so nice to offer, but I'll pull it together and I don't want you worrying about another thing."

"OK, honey. Just let me know if I can help with the party," she said. "I'll talk to you later."

chapter 12

In hindsight I see that for most of last summer, at least through George's departure, our lives essentially ran the normal course. Clara was playing and growing and doing well. George, so sharply focused on his work that he often seemed out of it, was in fact organized and productive and conscientious, even so far as being ready with a present for Clara's birthday. Not a thing was different with Lorraine except she had a beau, which you would think would have changed her life tremendously, but it didn't seem to. And as for me, I was my usual, somewhat confused, frantic self. I spent a few hours a week paying Mr. Stanley's bills, but I never seemed to be able to keep up with everything else even though my responsibilities weren't that great. The house was somewhat of a mess, and so was the barn; we ran out of things like milk or toilet paper; and being late seemed to be a matter of course for me. I never thought or planned ahead much except for worrying about keeping Clara consistently fueled, and the days ran into one another, one after another. My own lack of routine and discipline kept me from being productive, and a slight mental fog obfuscated any focus. I frittered away clear and useful thinking by occupying myself with interesting but purposeless reading and by talking with Joanie. The hazy and entertaining world of my wandering mind never had much connection with my day-to-day life in Hayden, and it definitely made for a strange overall disjointedness. I went through the motions of each day and, except for George, I thought no one seemed to know much about anything, or care.

chapter 13

Once I had more of a story, Joanie was fascinated by the Hayden murder. She asked for a full description of the fairgrounds and then wanted to know all about the social studies teacher. I didn't have much information about him, so we reveled in our own creations.

"Do you think he came down there to kill her?" Joanie asked.

"Who knows."

"He must have. What kind of social studies teacher—they're always meek, aren't they?—carries around a hunting knife?"

"… and in the summer."

"Ever!" she said. "I'm sorry but I really don't think a Toyota Camry and a hunting knife naturally go together. So there must be a psychopath involved." She paused. "No way."

"So what do you think he was thinking on the way down here?" I asked. "Not about the traffic."

"Oh ... he was probably listening to some cheap eighties band, like Duran Duran, what was that song, 'Hungry Like a Wolf'? Can't you just imagine him tapping his little, thin white fingers on the steering wheel, while he worried about what to say to the girl when he first saw her."

"I bet he was some annoyed when that Camry got all that dust on it on the way into the Bar 21," I said.

We went on inanely like that for a while. Then I moved the conversation to Lorraine.

"Guess what Lorraine's response to this was? The biggest thing to happen in Hayden in years, maybe in her lifetime, and she said, 'Honey, it's just pitiful.' That's it! And then on she went to her new sewing machine."

"I love it," said Joanie.

"Speaking of Lorraine ... guess what?"

"She won Mass Millions?" Joanie guessed.

"Nope. Oh, I better not tell you. It isn't fair."

"What?"

"I can't."

"Oh God. Are you going to tell me that *she* has a boy-friend?"

I was silent.

"C'mon! Are you freaking kidding me? Lorraine has a boyfriend—and I don't!"

I didn't say a word, delighted in the torture.

"How can this be?" Joanie laughed. "That's not fair! She's already had a husband! I've hardly even had a boyfriend. This can't be."

"It's true. Lorraine has a boyfriend. And he's cute, too."

"It's those legs," Joanie said. "She has those long thin legs! Mine are just too thick. I'm getting a personal trainer, or a plastic surgeon."

"They met at Mountain Vision."

"Receptionists have all the luck. I am not kidding you! Look at Swivel Elf—she's got boyfriends up the wazoo."

"Swivel Elf" is Joanie's name for her secretary. Swivel for the way she turns to talk as Joanie comes in and out of her office. And Elf because she's petite. I myself have never laid eyes on Swivel Elf.

"He's from the Midwest." I continued to talk about Tom even though Joanie was fully wrapped up in her own predicament.

"Wait a minute." That got her attention. "Did you say 'Midwest'?"

"Yes. Her boyfriend is from Ohio."

"Who cares then? God, that's a place I can totally do without! Lorraine can have him. I DO NOT want any kind of Western-type, Midwestern, whatever." She paused. "Unless, of course, he's George's long-lost twin or something."

"The admirable thing about you is how open-minded you are."

"Here's what I love about the West." Her voice was full of fun. "All there is to know is about one inch thick. Pioneers, cowboys, and Indians. A couple of wagon ruts in the grass and some Indian battles and there you have it—the whole story."

My laughter kept her going.

"Then, let's bring it up to today—national parks and, my personal favorite, water issues."

"You're forgetting Wal-Mart and RVs."

"Oh dear God. But my absolute first choice topic is *irrigation*. Can we please talk about that now?" Then pretending to make a demand of Swivel Elf, "Excuse me, could you please come in here right now and smash my head with a sledgehammer."

As we talked I had been walking around the house picking up laundry, putting away dishes, and generally trying to stay out of Clara's earshot without her noticing.

"Jesus, speaking of the West, I think I'm going to take Clara up to see the Custer Battlefield," I said.

"Have a ball," said Joanie. "You know, that is a great idea—take a six-year-old to the site of an Indian massacre! 'Look, honey, this is where the Indian was murdered, and right over there, here's where his pretty horse bled to death.'"

"Joanie, you seem to forget there isn't much else out here. I don't exactly have a choice between the Freedom Trail and Plymouth Rock!"

I heard a sigh at the other end of the line.

"Well, I hope you're going to tell me the battlefield is a mere five hours away."

"No, only two," I said. "And I don't have to dwell on the brutality with Clara; we can talk about the Indians being pushed off the land and all that. And by the way … it wasn't an Indian massacre."

"What?" she asked.

"The Battle of the Little Bighorn—it was the Indians who wiped out Custer, not the other way around."

"Oh yeah," she said. "I just forgot that for a minute."

I think it was at that point that we hung up because Joanie had to get to work and my portable phone was beeping again—low battery.

chapter 14

Clara and I pulled into the Custer Battlefield parking lot soon after it opened for the day. I thought there might be a chance we'd run into Tom. The sun was well above the groundswells to the east, but the heat wasn't bad yet. There's a time in the morning, a couple of hours after sunrise, when the temperature is perfect. Often, during those brief, glorious moments, I look straight up at the blue sky. With my head tipped back I can't see the grasslands or the sagebrush, and I imagine it's midday at the beach. In my mind I have a whole beautiful summer day ahead of me, sand and salt water nearby, and not an instant's dread of the oncoming heat.

Under an evergreen windbreak, I parked the truck. Lines of uniform white gravestones marched out before us from under the pine trees onto open ground. Clara climbed up front and put her arms out for sunscreen. I'm unrelenting about protecting her skin, so she has given up complaining. We had been singing songs a good bit of the way on the drive and I think we were on "American Pie" as I rubbed the cream onto her arms and across her tiny cheekbones.

"Mummy, look!" she said, pointing over my shoulder across the parking lot.

Just to the right of the visitors' center was a phone booth, and talking on the phone was Tom Baxter.

"It's Grammy's … It's Mr. Baxter!" Clara slid across the seat and began throwing the whole of her body weight into opening the heavy door.

"You wait just a cotton-pickin' minute!" I pulled her back. "Let's give him time to finish his phone call. Here, have some juice and eat these while you wait." I handed her some pretzels.

Even from across the parking lot, his expression seemed like what I had seen in the stands at the rodeo, sort of constricted and hard. Slowly tapping a fist against his thigh, he turned his face into the telephone. I got Clara singing "I've Been Working on the Railroad" to keep her inside the truck. But when she saw Tom hang up there was no stopping her. It must have been the ice cream cone he bought for her at the Rodeo picnic.

She jumped from the truck and yelled, "Hi, Mr. Baxter!"

He headed for his car, but when she yelled a second time, he turned around, puzzled. Then a smile spread across his face and he threw his arms open wide, bending a bit in the middle. How could she resist? (I could hardly resist.) And she ran right into his arms.

"Where's Grammy?" Clara asked.

"Where do you think?" Tom knew she'd come up with the answer.

"Working," they both said almost in unison.

Then Tom turned to me. "Would you mind some company?"

"We'd love it," I answered. "I was wondering if we might see you here."

"What do you say we ride out to the end first, to the Reno Battlefield?"

"Sure."

The three of us headed back to the truck.

The basic story of the Battle of the Little Bighorn is this: In the year 1876, the United States government ordered all the tribes of the Plains Indians to report to reservations at once. There they were to remain, but not all of them followed the orders. General George Armstrong Custer, a brash and ambitious Civil War hero, was sent with troops to see to it that those Indians holding out in eastern Wyoming and Montana surrendered their way of life and moved to the Dakota reservation. It was for that purpose that Custer and his men arrived at the Little Bighorn River in June 1876. Riding down ravines, through draws, and over the open swells, the Seventh U.S. Cavalry was surprised to come upon the biggest gathering ever of Lakota, Cheyenne, and Arapaho. The camp spread for miles along the Little Bighorn, a virtual city of some seven thousand Indians—seven thousand Indians determined to hold on to their traditional nomadic way of life. They were there under the leadership of Sitting Bull.

Custer divided his forces and he, with two hundred and twenty-five men, headed north, apparently to come at the Indian encampment from above. Not a single one of the cavalrymen who rode with Custer made it out alive.

This I had explained to Clara, as best I could, before we arrived.

With Tom in the passenger seat, and Clara behind us, we drove up the hill past the Last Stand Monument over the fresh blacktop snaking its way along a ridge. White, sometimes crooked grave markers spotted the grassy hillsides to indicate where soldiers fell.

"This is it in this part of the country—the big event. The site that can't be missed," Tom said. "But you know what, Custer himself's never interested me much." He looked out over the landscape.

"Really?" I said.

"No. Not at all. He was a showboat and an idiot. He made a stupid mistake and it cost him. Cost his men even more." Tom rubbed his cheeks with the thumb and fingers of his right hand.

"He was outnumbered, didn't know the land, and had no idea what he was up against. What a shock, he lost!" Then he turned to me and Clara. "Now, Major Reno, that's where the story is. He and Benteen survived and so did most of their men. For two days and two nights they were out here and they made it."

We came to a Park Service marker on the right side of the road and I must have slowed the truck because Tom said, "Let's skip these and go right to the end. It's easier to see it all if we come the way they did. They were coming from the Rosebud." He pointed to the southeast.

I remember thinking how fortunate we were to be there with someone who knew so much. And almost in the same moment I realized how lazy I'd been. How could I drive all the way up there to show my little girl something important and not even bother to learn more before I arrived? Did I really think that she, that either of us, would get anything out of this by just stumbling and shuffling around in the heat from one sign to another?

"Have you been here before?" I asked Tom.

"No." Behind his sunglasses I could see he was squinting at something in the distance.

"Then how do you know so much about it?"

"Books, of course!" He smiled a smile that showed he

knew his answer would please me. Then he reached to the backseat and gave Clara's knee a tickling squeeze.

"Books! Have you ever heard of 'em?" he teased. "Books!"

Clara squealed between laughs, "Yes! I've heard of books."

We drove the nearly four miles from the visitors' center to the Reno-Benteen Battlefield, passing from National Park Service land into Crow Agency, the present-day reservation. Sunlight glinted blindingly off the distant windshields of vehicles on the interstate. A fallen-down four-strand barbed-wire fence made its way down toward a dried-up riverbed, and a tiny set of dilapidated bleachers sat seemingly in the middle of nowhere. Missing from the land was the sagebrush and swaying prairie grass of the Park Service property. Instead, the reservation vegetation clipped short by grazing livestock was dotted with piles of manure and scraggly yucca. Horses standing a few ridges over to the east gave some scale to the vast expanse of land and sky.

At the hilltop where Reno and Benteen held out, there is now a parking lot. Cement and gravel walkways, so tame even wheelchairs can make the trip, cover the site. At first, when I got out of the truck with Tom and Clara, I was completely discouraged. Wherever you go, I thought, it's all the same—the Redwood Forest, Custer

Battlefield, the Everglades, Joshua Tree, and Acadia National Park. Just take the signs, the walkways, the parking lots, the placards, and Porta Pottis, and there you have it. The scenery and the words change, but how much does that even matter, after all, when most of us half read, half pay attention? It's as if we set aside these sites to make them all the same and say to ourselves, "Here's an important place—you don't have to know why, and there's certainly no reason to understand or feel anything about it, but since it has the predictable look of a national park, you know it must be important. Now, take that sixty-five-dollar Golden Eagle Pass of yours, and move on to the next one."

Then Tom began to talk about what happened all around us and my pessimism faded. We weren't with a group. We weren't listening to a guide who had repeated himself day after day. We didn't have the driving tour tape. We were there with a friend, someone who was genuinely interested, who knew something and who could tell a story.

"Right down there, up and down that river, were thousands of teepees. A whole city of Indians, thousands of men, women, and children all along that river." Tom pointed a stiff finger at the river valley below. "At first it was thought that the camp went for four miles along the river—the Indians called it Greasy Grass—but now they think it was only about two miles." He looked down at Clara, who was standing next to him. "Two miles is still pretty darn far. And up there"—he pointed to a flat bench of land to the west above the Indian campsite—"there were maybe twenty thousand ponies grazing."

Clara's eyes were wide.

"The Indians measured wealth in ponies, so they were rich."

He pointed east to where the cavalry came from and showed us where Custer split off and sent Major Reno in to attack the Indian camp. Reno and his men did as they were ordered, but were quickly outflanked by the warriors, and retreated to the hill where we were standing.

"The soldiers could hear screams and war cries from up north and they could see the smoke from the gunfire, but they didn't know what had happened to Custer. Once the Indians finished off Custer, they headed down here."

I looked at Clara. Her eyes were fixed on Tom's face.

Tom went on. "The Indians used guns they had taken from the dead soldiers. So they turned the cavalry's own weapons against them here. Indian warriors were all around this hill, shooting up at the soldiers. Soldiers got behind dead horses and mules to protect themselves."

Clara wrinkled her nose and said, "Eeewww."

Tom wasn't fazed. "Once it got dark the shooting stopped and the soldiers spent all night digging trenches for protection. They only had a few shovels, so they dug with whatever they had—knives, forks, and tin cups. In the morning the shooting began again. Reno ordered everyone to conserve bullets and leave the shooting only to those who could shoot the best. Those who weren't excellent shots were to supply the good shooters with loaded guns. A lot of the soldiers were immigrants, Irish mostly, and very few had any experience that counted.

"A doctor set up a field hospital"—he gestured to the south side of the hill—"for the wounded, who were all moaning for water. Everyone was thirsty, and some of the soldiers even put rocks in their mouths to make saliva. The doctor knew the wounded would die in the heat if they didn't soon get something to drink."

My curly hair was all tied up in an elastic and the sun was beginning to roast the back of my neck.

"So a group of soldiers braved the gunfire and snuck down to the river for water," Tom explained. "Only one guy got shot, and he lived. All of the soldiers who went for water later were given Medals of Honor."

Tom pulled a light blue handkerchief from his pocket and wiped his brow. It must have been a matter of habit, because any perspiration evaporated right away in the parched air.

"The soldiers defended themselves all that next day, and then the soldiers were surprised to see the Indians packing up their enormous camp and heading for the Bighorns." He looked off to the blue mountains to the west. "They thought it was a trick and stayed ready for an attack all that night. But the next day, another group of soldiers came along from the north and assured the survivors that it was all over. The Indians were gone. And so was Custer."

And so passed the hours of our morning.

Back near the visitors' center, we walked the paths among sagebrush and the mariposa lilies, Clara skipped ahead and around, and my conversation with Tom drifted naturally from one topic to another—books, articles, people. I don't remember all that we talked about, but I do know he asked me a lot about George. He was curious to know how George had first become interested in paleontology. I told Tom the story of George, at ten years old, with his father, at the Hayden park by the Old Courthouse. George was playing down by the creek, throwing sticks into the water and running along the banks to keep up as the twigs rushed downstream. He bent over to pick up a big stick and there at his feet was something that looked like a bone. It was about two feet long and gray, with more of the feeling of a rock than a bone. George was certain it was a dinosaur bone. He brought it home and put it on top of his dresser, telling everyone it was a real dinosaur bone. Lorraine and George Sr. humored him for a while and then told him it was just a cow bone or something and he should let up talking about it. But George was insistent. He wrote a letter to the president of the University of Wyoming telling him that he knew he had found a dinosaur bone and asked how could he prove it. The university president, to his great credit, wrote right back and invited George to visit him in Laramie with his find. They would take the bone to the science department to determine once and for all if it was from a dinosaur. What could Lorraine and George Sr. do? They drove the six hours to Laramie with little George and his bone. Sure enough, it was real—a seventy-five-million-year-old thighbone of a Troodon!

He was right and he was hooked.

It's a story that's hard to believe, but true, and I could tell Tom appreciated it in the right way. Most people miss that. They think it was just George's great luck to be the one to find the dinosaur bone. Or then there's Lorraine's perspective, which is that it was an important moment because it put one of her kids on the front page of the *Hayden Press*. But Tom was different. I remember he said, "Just think how many other people probably saw that bone before George, sitting right out in the open at the town park. It took a certain kind of kid to see it for what it was and then follow through."

Maybe it was just wishful thinking on my part, but I thought he recognized in the story George's character—his confidence, his determination and persistence even among doubters, his single-mindedness and the depth of his interest. It was reassuring and affirming to have a little bit of company in my appreciation of George.

Then he asked me about meeting George and I told him the story of the train ride in New York and how I borrowed George's jacket.

He interrupted, "What were you reading?"

"What?" I asked. I was used to telling the story, because people often wonder how I got way out here and why my path ever crossed George's. But I wasn't used to anything beyond the initial "How did you two meet?"

"You said you were reading on the train. What were you reading?" he repeated.

I thought a few seconds. "*Angle of Repose*. Wallace Stegner." Then I smiled and said, "Phew. I passed! That was fifteen years ago."

Tom smiled, nodding his head, and said, "No, I knew you'd remember. When something's important, you do remember the details."

On the way back up a ravine to the visitors' center, Tom walked beside or behind me. When we had been going downhill he walked in front—the gentlemanly thing to do in case a lady were to slip. When there were brief lulls in conversation, he absentmindedly sang the words to a song I couldn't make out. Clara was unpredictable, running ahead and then holding back. Our talk made its way back to Major Reno, the fear he must have felt, and anger, too. We talked about how that whole world of the cavalry and the Indians is now entirely gone. The sky, the wind, and the weather are the same and the bones remain. The horseshoes are there and the buttons, but the world and the culture in which those people lived is completely gone now. And it wasn't really that long ago. Tom said, "No, it wasn't long ago, and the older I get, the more recent it seems!"

I remember that line, because at that moment I felt so many questions about Tom's life surge up inside me. It was like they were at the top of my chest, ready to roll. But I held back, remembering my promise to myself not to pry, and I know I also held back as a small tribute to George and his Western sense of letting things lie.

Inside the visitors' center we casually separated, each of us looking at the display cases. In 1983 there was an enormous grass fire that raged across the battlefield, clearing the area of the dense native groundcover and exposing many artifacts. The visitors' center is full of what was found during the ensuing archaeological survey—

loading levers of Remington revolvers, cartridge cases, wedding rings, tobacco tags, coins, spurs, and of course, arrowheads. I had a split-second thought of wishing George were an archaeologist rather than a paleontologist. Human artifacts are so much more accessible for my imagination than fossils. I knew I'd keep that thought to myself, though.

As we walked from case to case, the fatigue that overwhelms me every time I'm in a museum of any kind hit me hard. I couldn't help overhearing a conversation off to my left. We had seen the two men from a distance earlier in the day out by Reno's hill. Bearded and short in stature, they were both dressed in full U.S. Cavalry regalia. They were talking to a large young woman from the Park Service. In heavy Scottish accents the men described how thrilled they were to see the Custer Battlefield at last, and yes, they were there for the reenactment scheduled for later that day. Their enthusiasm and excitement were almost unbelievable.

The heavy-lidded Park Service ranger asked, "So, where are you folks from?"

"Edinburgh."

I could see the threesome out of the corner of my eye. Apparently the heavy Scottish accents meant not a thing to her.

"Edinburgh ... Scotland," one of the men explained.

"Oooooh! Scotland. Geez, that's a long way away. Must be real different over here."

"Oh yes, yes it is," one of the soldiers responded.

"Real different," she repeated, with special emphasis on the "real."

She was just so big and fleshy and shapeless and they were so small and trim. She looked down at them and they up at her. Something about the whole combination was exhausting.

There was a bit of silence and then one of the men picked up the slack. "Where are you from?"

The happy girl was eager to answer. "Oh, I'm from clear down in Greeley."

Then it dawned on her that they might not know where Greeley was. "Greeley, Colorado."

Sounds of understanding out of the Scotsmen.

Then she hit the nail on the head. "It's real different up here. Real different."

I couldn't take any more, so I moved Clara along to the bookstore.

When we got outside, back into the boiling day, Tom was exasperated. "Did you happen to hear the conversation in there between the two cavalrymen and the Park Service woman?"

"Yes! Thank God you heard it, too. That was priceless," I said.

"Can you imagine? For God's sake, those guys came *all the way* from Scotland to see this and all she could say is 'It must be REAL different'!! Forget about the fact that there they were, standing right in front of her, dressed as Reno and Benteen. She probably doesn't even know who Reno was!" He was laughing, but mad, too.

"Who were those guys?" Tom's voice was forceful. "I know a lot of Europeans get into this stuff, but why on earth would those two Scotsmen in particular have such an interest in the Battle of Little Bighorn? Where did they get the uniforms? Are they going anywhere else? Is there anything special they want to see? Any particular interests? Jesus, people are unbelievable! I just wanted to take that idiotic woman and kick her stupid, fat ass right out the door!"

Clara, who was by then holding Tom's hand, giggled.

I tried my best to imitate the ranger's voice. "Well now, that would be REAL different."

Tom tipped his head back and howled with laughter. And that was the moment. That was when I thought, Here is a kindred spirit. Here is my drink of water in the desert. Here is someone who can appreciate George with me, who can be mad with me and see the humor in all that's wrong with the world, and here is someone who is interested. Here could be a real friend.

It was only eleven o'clock in the morning, but we decided to get lunch before heading back to Hayden. Just before you get on the interstate is the Custer Battlefield Trading Post, where you can get French fries and cheap Indian trinkets. And surprisingly, behind the counter in glass cases are a few real Indian treasures—beaded war shirts, saddlebags, baby moccasins.

Tom paid for our lunch. Clara and I each had grilled cheese sandwiches and French fries with ketchup. Tom ordered a hamburger and ate only the meat, leaving the white bun on the side of his plate.

After we finished eating we browsed a bit in the shop. At one point Tom and I found ourselves looking at the famous portrait of Sitting Bull, the one near the end of the great chief's life where he sits regally defeated in his buckskins, with a single feather in his hair. Braids, beads, and necklaces hang from his neck, and right there in the middle of his torso, as plain as day, is Jesus on the cross. I commented on the crucifix; I don't remember exactly what I said, but something like it seemed strange that Sitting Bull would wear it. Tom said the cross was probably given to Sitting Bull by the missionary he liked, Father DeSmet, "Black Robe."

The incongruity of Sitting Bull with the crucifix reminded me of seeing Tom in the Hayden stands the week before, crossing himself right in the middle of the rodeo.

"You're Catholic, aren't you?" I asked Tom.

"No. Why do you ask?"

"That night at the rodeo, I saw you do the sign of the cross."

"Nope. Not me. Musta been someone else."

He raised his gray eyebrows and gave me a devilish little smile.

Just then, before I could say a word, Clara came out from behind a row of crowded shelves carrying a tiny porcelain Indian girl with long black braids and a buckskin dress.

"Well, would you look at that beautiful doll!" Tom turned on the heel of his boot and held his hand out to Clara. "You should have something to help you remember the day, sweetheart. Here, let me get her for you."

Clara beamed.

Tom quickly paid for the doll at the register near the door. A solidly built woman in tourist clothes, about my age, looked at our group. She waited for a saleswoman to get something from the jewelry case, but her eyes fixed on us. She looked puzzled, and I was sure she must have been trying to figure out our situation—father, daughter, and granddaughter? Older man, young girlfriend, and daughter? I looked away and thought, How could she ever understand?

Next to the front door of the trading post, on our way out, a fancy engraved brass plaque caught my eye. It said:

ON THIS SITE IN 1897
NOTHING HAPPENED

chapter 15

Clara and I headed straight back to Hayden. I needed to get to Mr. Stanley's office to pick up the checkbook and ledger before the doors were locked. After working for him for I don't know how many years, I still don't have a key to the Stanley office. I don't mind. Mr. Stanley likes Christopher, his butler of sorts, to lock and unlock the office, and that's fine by me. Everyone has eccentricities, and the old man just has a few extra. I'm grateful he lets me take the books home when George is away, so I don't always have to have a babysitter for Clara.

On the side of the highway stood a billboard I'd never noticed before with an enormous picture of a handsome cowboy sitting on a hay bale. He looked up at a smaller version of himself, a young boy in a cowboy hat. Above their heads in large type were the words "Real Men Don't Abuse Women. Talk to Your Sons."

The message could have been anywhere, but the cowboy hats and hay bales made me wonder, Where the hell am I?

Thankfully, Clara was so busy jabbering on about her birthday that she didn't notice. It was a sign I didn't feel like explaining to a six-year-old.

chapter 16

There were two messages on the answering machine when we got home.

The first was Joanie:

"I guess you're not back yet? Was it ever so fascinating? You must be thirsty and I bet your lips are SO chapped." Thirst and chapped lips are the two things Joanie remembers most from her one visit to Wyoming. "Two pieces of important news—first, Whitey Bulger is NOT the man for me after all. I completely forgot he loves dogs! How I forgot such an important fact, I can't begin to imagine."

She took a deep breath.

"Crime I can take, but dog hair—no way. So, he's now officially out of the running. Second, I have a date tonight and it's not a dating service date. Can you believe it? Set up by someone in my office. Dear Swivel Elf is all a-twitter.

"I have meetings all afternoon … call you when I can."

I hit the delete button.

Next was George:

"Hi, sweet things. I'm sooo sad you're not there! I just want to hear your voices. Everything is going well here. We're headed out into the field now, and I'm not sure when I'll be able to call again. It'll be soon, I think. I hope you're having fun. Clara"—his voice turned sing-songy—"not counting today, only eighteen more days till your birthday! I miss you guys. I love you."

I saved George's message. I always do. It's oddly morbid, I realize, but I want a record of his voice just in case I never hear from him again. You never know.

The house was extra hot because the sun had been beating in through the windows all morning. Stupidly, I forgot to close the windows and pull the shades before we left. Clara, happy to be home, went straight to work making miniature clay food for her dolls. Why is it that kids never seem to notice the heat? I tried for a bit to work on Mr. Stanley's payroll, but quickly decided to wait for the clearer thinking that comes with the cool of the nights. I just had to finish it in time to return the books to the office sometime the next day. Since the house was a furnace, I told Clara I was going to the barn where it's shady, and if there's any breeze at all, you feel it there.

Usually I hear if a car pulls up, but sometimes in the

summer, with the fans all going, I don't. That's what must have happened that afternoon, because suddenly there was a knock at the front door, a door we never use. Percy bolted through the house, barking up a storm.

There stood Tom, holding my raggedy old watch in front of his face.

"My watch!" I said, and at the same time he asked, "Missing something?" He held his free hand out to Percy, who had already calmed down.

"Thank you!" Then I qualified with a laugh, "Well, I didn't really miss it all that much, but George will certainly thank you."

I gestured for him to come in. Somehow he seemed taller inside. Maybe the house was just too crowded with stuff or maybe it was his solid, straight stance. In an instant my mind registered all that was around us—Clara's nests and clay spread over the dining room table, piles of laundry from the line (at least it was folded) on the couch, mail heaped on the coffee table, fans on chairs in odd places with their cords stretched inconveniently across the room, and the bookcase, much too haphazardly loaded. Suddenly I was self-conscious and nervous and I wanted Tom Baxter out of our chaos. He wasn't the kind of person who didn't pay attention to things.

"You didn't find that today," I said.

"No. I didn't." There was the devilish little smile again.

"When did you?" I asked. "Where was it?"

"When and where do *you* think?"

"Oh, come on! Just tell me." He didn't answer. "Is this some sort of quiz?"

Tom shrugged his shoulders.

"OK, let me think." I put my hands in my messy hair and tipped my head back. "When did I notice it was missing.... You found it in the grass at the park after the Rodeo parade!"

"That's pretty good," he said, "but not quite right. Not quite as observant as I thought you were. What kind of car do I drive?"

"Oh, for God's sake! A white car ..." I thought a minute. "An Oldsmobile."

"What kind of Oldsmobile?"

"I have *no idea*!" I said with a laugh. "How 'bout them apples? I have no idea!"

His eyebrows raised in a mischievous look.

Enjoying the banter, I said, "So, are you going to tell me about my watch or not?"

"I guess so. I found it on the sidewalk where we all watched the parade."

"I was *very* close, then! Give me a little credit."

"Close, but not right." He smiled. "It was a good test."

"Judging from the mess I live in, I'm pretty amazed I knew what month I'd lost it in!"

I don't remember if he responded because I was more concerned with getting out of the house. I asked Tom if he wanted to see the barn. We walked by the big table. I closed Mr. Stanley's checkbook and he gave Clara a little tickle. She flinched, but didn't move from her project.

Before we went out the back door, I filled a bucket with hot water in the kitchen sink to take to the barn.

"Screen's got a hole in it," Tom said.

I laughed. What else could I do? "Screen's got a hole, dryer's broke, as they say, and the washing machine will be next, thresholds are missing, house needs paint, and the whole place is a holy mess! A good mess," I qualified, "but a mess, all except the barn. Wait till you see how I have that under control."

Inside the barn, the heat wasn't as bad. I went to the stall and brought Timmy out onto the cement floor and put him on the cross ties. Tom watched as if he was witnessing something utterly foreign. I pulled George's old plastic lawn chair from the feed room and set it a few feet in front of Timmy.

"Here, you sit and watch."

Tom sat down, took off his straw cowboy hat, set it

in his lap, and rubbed his head, relaxed. It was the first time I'd seen him without a hat. He'd tipped it before, but never taken it all the way off. His hair was gray, not white, and grew straight back in fine, straight strands off of his forehead. It wasn't a full head of hair really, but it wasn't thin, either. For the first time he really looked old to me. I was immediately reminded of a moment in the dim light of my grandparents' library when I suddenly saw my grandfather in a different way and realized he was truly an old man.

I went quietly and assuredly about my business; getting clean wraps and folded cotton from a plastic bin, a sterilized syringe, Epsom salts for the soak bucket, and ointment from the little refrigerator in the tack room. Thick ointment turns to liquid in the heat of the summer. I pushed aside Clara's juice, pulled two bottles of Budweiser from the fridge, and opened them on an opener George nailed to the barn wall years ago.

I handed Tom the beer and took a sip of mine before putting it down on the cement floor next to the wall.

"Don't mind if I do," he said. "Must be five o'clock back east, by now."

I looked at my watch. "Past five in Massachusetts, but not quite five in Ohio, in case you happen to call *that* 'back east.'"

"Oh well." He tipped the bottle back.

As Timmy's leg soaked, I brushed his spotted coat and completely combed out his feathery tail. Tom asked all about the pony and what had happened to his leg and how I knew about horses. I told him about my childhood in New England and how I was one of those girls who spent every free moment at the barn because I could never get enough of horses. As I worked and spoke it occurred to me how strange and wonderful it was to talk about all that again. It seemed no one asked me anything anymore. George used to, but now we both think we know everything about each other, so much so that we talk about the past hardly at all. And as for Lorraine, forget it. With most everyone, for that matter, it's as if everything is as it is and for no particular reason whatsoever. Joanie asks me things, but it's from a distance, always on the phone.

All the nervous self-consciousness I felt when Tom was in the house was gone in the barn. We passed an hour or so like that—me working and Tom sitting asking questions, occasionally humming or singing a song, and slowly rubbing Percy's black and white head. The dog watched Tom's every move, as Border collies tend to do, but the petting seemed to calm them both.

As I began wrapping Timmy's leg, Tom brought up Clara's health. "Lorraine tells me Clara has a very serious medical problem."

"She does," I said. "Medium chain acyl-CoA dehy-drogenase deficiency. MCADD."

"As I understand it, she needs a steady supply of food or she'll have a seizure. Is that right?" he asked.

"That's pretty much it," I said. "She lacks the enzyme that allows her to use stored energy—fat—so if she doesn't eat, or if she can't keep food down because of a virus or something, she can have a seizure or worse, go into a coma or die."

"Jesus." He shook his head. He was quiet for a moment, then said, "What a responsibility."

Kneeling by Timmy, I tied the bandage, then stood up. "Yup."

"I'm sure you're doing everything you can, but is the hospital out here good enough for her?" he asked. "Do they know what the hell they're doing?"

"I've worried about that, but I really think it's fine. The amazing, lucky thing is that they were able to diagnose it in the first place when she was tiny. That's when it's the most dangerous, when people don't know what the problem is. But now that we know, it's really pretty simple; any hospital could handle it because all she really needs is an IV with glucose."

Tom nodded slowly as he listened.

"It's really more of a question of me handling it," I said. "I'm the one who better be watching her all the time and if there's a problem get her to the hospital fast."

"Will she outgrow it?"

"No. Not really. But it will get easier to handle as she gets older. I guess that after puberty the body is better overall at regulating itself and she'll begin to have a better sense of when she needs to eat. So it won't go away, but it should get better."

"You've got a big job," he said. "But you know, try as you might, you can't always protect them."

I thought of Tom's son's body, dead in the car after the accident. "I know," I said.

"She'll disappoint you sometime, Kate. She will. But do your goddamnedest not to disappoint her. And you know what else?" He straightened up in his chair. "Don't just feed her and wash her clothes and drive her around and assume she knows what's important to you. Do more for her than that."

"What do you mean?"

"Show her what matters to you and be sure she gets it. Teach her!"

I nodded.

"Oh, now I'm preaching," he said, putting his hat back on.

"Good!" I said. "I need it! Give me more."

"Nope. That's enough." He stood up.

I put Timmy in the stall and walked Tom to his car. On the way out I allowed myself a question on another subject. "Where are you staying?"

"When Lorraine won't have me, I'm at the Lariat, across from Jiffy Lube."

I nodded, but couldn't quite picture him there.

"They have weekly rates and the rooms are clean." He paused. "I'm looking for a place to rent, though."

I couldn't resist another one, so I asked, "You're staying?"

"We'll see. But I'm sure thinking about it." He put his hand on the door handle and looked over at me with an easy grin. "It's a better place than most … and the company's going to be tough to beat."

I didn't want him to leave, not at all, not Hayden and not my house right then, but I said nothing.

He reached in his pocket and coins jingled. He pulled out a handful and picked one from the top.

"Don't take any wooden nickels," he said, pushing a coin into the palm of my hand. "And don't ever say I never did anything for ya!"

I smiled and looked down at the coin in my hand—a 1908 Indian head ten-dollar piece.

His white Oldsmobile Cutlass Sierra was parked under the old silver poplar tree in our side yard. Just as he got into the driver's seat Tom said the tree was spectacular. He'd never seen leaves like that before, dark green on the top with snow white undersides. I said I thought it was beautiful, too, like two entirely different trees all in one, but people around here say they're only trash trees. I wondered how far west you started to find silver poplars, since Tom hadn't seen one in Ohio.

chapter 17

I had a dream that night about gliding across New England farmland in a horse-drawn sleigh. There were snow-covered trees, post and rail fences, stone walls, and bloodred cardinals flying about. In the distance stood a single, perfect white steeple. It was my hometown, and nothing could have been more familiar to me, even though I've spent hardly any time there for well over twenty years. In the dream I was the age I am now, early forties, only it was taking place during those idyllic years when I was about eleven or twelve, when my father was still well, Mother hadn't yet begun to drive me crazy, and my grandparents were alive. Joanie would have just graduated from college. The air was crisp and clean and my childhood friends were all around me, laughing and singing and, of course, whispering. Lorraine was there, too, chatting incessantly about Christmas decorations and cross-stitchery. I was mad that she didn't seem to notice how different from Hayden everything was or that she was riding along with people she didn't know. I interrupted her detailed description of how one could make darling Christmas carolers out of bowling pins to shout, "Lorraine, this is where I grew up! This is where I am from. These are my friends." I stood in the sleigh and pointed across the frozen mill pond, my voice getting louder with every word. "That is where my grandparents live! My great-grandparents lived here, too, and their parents before them! Another great-grandfather came to this town from Ireland. Did you know that? The library is right over there. That's the old road to Boston! People have been using that route for almost four hundred years. Did you even know I grew up near Boston?"

I could feel my face twisting. "Do you see? Do you see how different this is? Do you understand what this means to me? Don't you ever wonder about me? Wonder anything?"

Then Clara was in the sleigh with us, too. Either I hadn't noticed her or she just appeared, but she said with force, "Mummy! Don't!"

Lorraine stared wide-eyed, as if she might have been afraid of me. Then suddenly we stopped short in the deep snow. The white pony lurched forward and the whole front of the sleigh broke away. The pony was free with reins and shafts dragging behind him, and the sleigh, with all of us in it, sat as still as a boulder in the middle of the field.

A sleigh really did break once when I was little and that was the end of the ride. I remember not being upset at all because in my child-mind, I thought life would be filled with so many horse-drawn sleigh rides over open fields. All the time in my future there would be beautiful adventures in ever more picturesque settings.

But in my dream, we were devastated. My friends fussed and cried. I twittered in confusion. Then Lorraine stood up, pulled from her coat pocket a crafter's hot-glue gun, picked up the pieces, and happily put it all back together. She called to the pony, who came trotting right back.

"Let's just keep going," she said, wrapping her arm affectionately around my shoulder.

I couldn't say a word, but we were off again. And Lorraine, of all people, saved the day.

chapter 18

The next ten days passed rather uneventfully. Hour followed hour and day followed day. Giant thunderheads, white and deep gray rising high above the plains, built in the afternoons. We heard rumbling, but not a drop of rain fell—not once. As August approached, the daylight hours shortened ever so slightly, but it didn't go unnoticed by me. Any amount of time with less sun blazing was a welcome change in my book. The hope of fall wouldn't be that far off.

I took care of Clara, the animals, the house, and paid the Rafter T Ranch bills. I also began working on a special project for Mr. Stanley—an inventory of his house, barns, and guesthouse. He must have wanted it done for his estate planning, or maybe he just wanted to be able to look at the list and literally take stock of his possessions. He didn't tell me why and I didn't ask. It would take me until the end of the year or longer, I knew, but according to Mr. Stanley, there was no rush whatsoever.

So I began in late July, with clipboard in hand, counting monogrammed silver forks, measuring frames and noting the location of signatures, and checking first-edition books for copyright dates. With the books I had to take myself in hand to keep to the job of documenting—no reading, no browsing. As usual, Mr. Stanley stayed in his darkened bedroom and I saw him not at all. I directed all my questions to Christopher, the balding, blond butler, of sorts, and Mr. Stanley's all-around right-hand man. All I know about Christopher is that he's from Florida, misses his aged mother, hates exercise of any kind, and generally has little use for Hayden. He always walks with his chin up, except when he has indigestion, which seems to be most of the time, and he giggles a bit too often. I probably tried to imagine it all to be more interesting than it was to entertain myself. In the least the project was a diversion.

The first two times I went to Mr. Stanley's to start the inventory, our neighbor Casey came to babysit. Birthday anticipation enveloped Clara more and more every day. I've never been very good at parties, let alone at putting one on, so I totally avoided talking about her big day, August 5. At almost seven years old Clara's sense of time was still enviable. She was free and unencumbered, not that different from our dog, Percy, in many ways. It seemed as if it wouldn't matter one bit if George were away for two days or two months, she just knew Daddy was away and Daddy would come back.

As for me, I missed George. My feelings about his absence rose and fell in a predictable pattern. The first few days were the hardest and the longest, then I became sort of accustomed to his being gone and confident in my ability to handle our lives alone. Then came the annoyance, and my annoyance was building.

George and I did have a few nice telephone calls, so I had some idea of what he was doing in Kemmerer. But as the time went on the conversations seemed to be shorter and shorter. He usually called me when he was too tired to talk, or when one of us was running out the door. I often hung up the phone feeling worse, not better, for having spoken to him. Strangely, I didn't mention a word to George about Tom, not about the trip to the Custer Battlefield, not about Tom's visit to our house. Nothing. I knew it was odd, but the subject didn't come naturally, so I didn't say anything.

Joanie's date, the one she mentioned on the answering machine, was a disaster. He had a thick gold chain and blow-dried hair.

I don't think I spoke to Lorraine at all during those ten days. She hardly ever calls when George is away, and I guess I don't call her much, either. I wondered about her more often than usual, but that was really because I wondered about Tom.

I thought of Tom quite a bit and even considered dropping by the Lariat motel to say hello. I wanted to spend more time with him, but as usual, didn't want to push myself on anyone. It occurs to me now that this might seem as if it were building into some sort of love interest for me. It wasn't—not at all. In Tom I think I saw a potential friend, a real friend, but I was also just plain curious. I couldn't help it, and at heart he seemed like a talker. How did he bring himself to keep going after losing his wife and son? Does he miss Ohio? What was his house like? Does he have brothers and sisters? Anyone? Whom did he call on the telephone? What was the strained expression at the rodeo and in the phone booth at the Custer Battlefield? Why had he crossed himself if he wasn't Catholic, and why on earth did he say he didn't cross himself when he most certainly did?

chapter 19

In a small town you run into people you know all the time. Familiar faces are everywhere. So it wasn't a big surprise to run into Tom and Lorraine. What was surprising was where. Clara and I were at Shipton's Big R, a ranch supply store out by the interstate. It's an enormous fluorescent-lighted box of a store where they sell everything for the ranch from round pen panels and fencing, to shotguns, to Western wear. I could easily load up on things for the barn like new brushes and buckets and a hose. But I only allowed myself to buy what we really couldn't do without until we had a few things taken care of around the house—namely a new washer and dryer. Anyway, I had paste wormer tubes for the horses and just needed to get a bag of dog food for Percy, when I heard giggling over by the dressing rooms.

There in front of the mirrors stood a striking Lorraine. Tom, off to the side behind a rack of pants, was watching her intently. She looked prettier than I think

I had ever seen her, with color in her cheeks and a face that was simply alive. Dressed from head to toe in cowgirl clothes—black lace-up ropers on her feet, a pair of dark Rockies—the kind of jeans with a yolk in front and back and no back pockets—Lorraine's sixty-three-year-old figure was smashing! Around her smaller-than-I-would-have-expected waist was a black belt with a big silver buckle. On top she wore a red and white flowered Western shirt with faux mother-of-pearl-covered snaps. Lorraine was a Western vision. Tom held a black felt hat in his hands, ready for her to try.

In the seconds it took Clara and me to make our way over to the dressing rooms, I suddenly felt self-conscious and grubby in my T-shirt and old shorts.

"Well, look at you!" I said.

Lorraine spun around, blushing.

"Oh, honey!" She laughed. "Can you believe him!"

Clara hugged Lorraine around the tops of her legs.

"Can I believe him?" I said. "You! You look fabulous!"

"I don't know if I've ever had clothes on like this before!" she exclaimed.

"A Wyoming girl should dress like a Wyoming girl," Tom said with a smile. "Doesn't she look wonderful?"

"She sure does," I said.

"She wants to go to the prime rib supper at the Elks

tonight and there's dancing afterward," said Tom. "But I can't learn to two-step with a girl in pearls. I need a cowgirl! So I made the decision yeste'day mornin', we'd have to go shopping!'"

Before I left them, Tom said, "Hey, Kate, I saw a book on your shelf, *The Lance and the Shield*, and I was wondering if you might let me borrow it?"

I must have hesitated or something because he went on, "If you don't like to lend books, I *completely* understand. I'll just see if the library has it."

"No, no," I said. "The biography of Sitting Bull? You can borrow it anytime. I was just trying to think of where it is."

"In the bookcase in your living room," he said. "Second shelf, over to the right."

"For God's sake, you were in my house for less than five minutes and you know it better than I do!" I kidded.

"He is something!" Lorraine joined in. "The other day I had my vehicle serviced and I needed to give the man my license plate number. I went to go look at the car and Tom started justa rattlin' the darn thing off."

"County three, five-four-three E," Tom said.

"See what I mean! Sure as sugar, I'll never know that number as long as I live!" Lorraine was having fun. "Do you know yours, honey?"

"Of course not!" I said.

"Three, seven-one-eight-two," Tom said, showing off and enjoying it. "What do you say I pick that book up tomorrow?"

"Anytime," I said. "I should be around all day."

That was about all there was to it. In the parking lot was Lorraine's spotless Ford Explorer. I wondered where they would go next and what they would talk about. The whole day was theirs. And the night, and tomorrow, too. Then for a moment I wished I were Lorraine. Isn't it the young most people envy? Aren't we a nation covetous of youth and future? Not me. No way. I look at my little Clara and think, Oh my Lord, you have such a long way to go. I have a long way to go, too. But Lorraine and Tom, they'd already made it through so much—so much work and so much loss and so much responsibility—and here they were having a ball together, free as birds. I wanted to be one of them.

On the way home James Taylor's "Fire and Rain" came on the radio. I hadn't heard it in so long, but every word came back to me and I sang along like a champ, trying to bring myself out of Lorraine's life and back into my own.

Clara, who had been looking out the window at a herd of antelope in the irrigated hayfields by the college, turned her attention silently to me. I'll never forget the strange expression on her face. It made me determined to get every single word of the song right because I knew exactly what she was feeling. She couldn't believe I knew a song she'd never even heard. The look was puzzled and maybe even slightly disapproving, and it meant that in my singing of the song, which I knew so well and she didn't at all, she somehow realized that I'd had a life before her—that I was a person before she was. I thought of something F. Scott Fitzgerald wrote: "For the young can't believe in the youth of their fathers." Somehow Clara couldn't believe that everything about me wasn't hers. She didn't know all there was to know about me, after all. The moment was brief and then it was over.

Sometimes you see major turning points in your life from a mile away, like a graduation or a marriage or the birth of a child. Often they are celebrated with a party or ritual, or acknowledged with grief and mourning, but sometimes the important moment passes unnoticed, at least for a while. The turning point of the summer happened to me that day, and it was none of the above. It hit me seemingly out of the blue, at a mundane moment, and it came about only from the wanderings of my mind and a chance train of thought. Snippets of conversations, bits of knowledge, and a few odd thoughts bumped into one another and gave rise to an idea, a possibility really, that had never occurred to me before.

I was on the back porch, pouring Percy's dog food

into the big storage can. James Taylor was still playing in my head. I thought of Lorraine and Tom at Shipton's and of the way he said, "I need a cowgirl! So I made the decision yeste'day mornin', we'd have to go shopping!" He didn't say "yesterday morning" the way James Taylor says it. He said "yeste'day mornin'," as if there were no "r" in the word "yesterday." I was surprised I hadn't noticed that before because it's the way my mother says "yesterday," and my grandfather, and lots of people I know back home.

I watched as the brown nuggets of foul-smelling dog food hit the bottom of the can with a bang. My mind drifted from Tom's pronunciation to a question about myself—why do I even like dogs? They're work, and they're hairy, and they can be gross. But I do like dogs. I do. My father liked dogs. George likes dogs. Tom was particularly nice to Percy, so he must like dogs. Christ, even Whitey Bulger likes dogs!

Yesterday, yeste'day. Tom likes dogs, Whitey likes dogs. The night at the rodeo Tom wore a baseball hat and sunglasses. Hadn't I seen pictures of Whitey Bulger in a baseball hat and sunglasses again and again in the *Boston Globe*? The Indian head ten-dollar piece; Jesus, doesn't Whitey Bulger have an interest in coins?

The empty dog food bag fell to the floor and I stood up ramrod-straight. What if Tom Baxter *is* Whitey Bulger?

He could be. Conversations with Joanie came rushing back.... Whitey can't be without a woman.... He likes history ... books ... dogs ... coins. My mind was racing and my breathing came fast. Things I'd heard or read, information most people in Massachusetts know, came rushing to the fore. Wasn't Tom about the same age as Whitey, and the same build? And Tom with the license plates, didn't I read somewhere that Whitey had a gift with numbers? Did I? Was that true? No, he couldn't be Whitey. Tom is kind and he's from Ohio and he lost his son. He's not a gangster or a killer. He's not. He couldn't be. Or could he? Maybe. No. But why on earth would he say "yesterday" with a Boston accent? Jesus. Are there silver poplar trees in Ohio? Or any trees with leaves like that? God, I don't know.

The idea that Tom Baxter could be Whitey Bulger is the kind of thought that might race in and then immediately out of one's mind in a flash—not the kind of idea that should take on a life of its own, perpetuating itself.

I put my hands over my eyes and thought, This is crazy. I'm crazy!

chapter 20

I could almost hear the blood pulsing past my ears and through my head. I must not have said anything to Clara—I don't even know if she was inside the house, or out—I just marched off the back porch and started walking to the barn, to the clothesline, back to the barn again. Pacing and likely talking to myself, I saw nothing, felt nothing, smelled nothing, as if all my senses were blocked by thoughts too rampant and overwhelming.

Like a drill sergeant I rattled off, out loud or in my head, I'm not sure which, all I could think of about Whitey Bulger.

Irish. Boston. Southie. He's smart. He's loyal. He reads. I saw his FBI wanted poster once and it said right there something like, "Bulger is an avid reader with an interest in history. He is known to frequent libraries and historic sites." He's been jailed only once—for bank robbery—years ago. Alcatraz. His IQ was so high the CIA used him for a study while he was in prison. And yes, I think he does have a numbers kind of mind. He himself used prison time to study generals and criminals from the past—how they led and how they got caught and what mistakes they made. He's never been caught again. He's protective. He's kind. Ruthless. Charming. Careful. Disciplined, physically and mentally. The kind of man who would help an old lady across the street or buy an ice cream cone for a child, but would beat the hell out of a guy wasting time hanging out on the street corner. Didn't he win a big Mass Millions jackpot once?

Would he hurt Lorraine? Jesus! No, Whitey wouldn't hurt a woman, not unless she was a threat to him. No. Lorraine would never be a threat; how could she possibly? She takes everything at face value, no questions asked.

I dug both hands into my hair until my fingers reached the scalp at the crown of my head. Then taking two big handfuls of coarse hair, I pulled at it until it hurt.

What did Whitey look like? I tried to remember clippings Joanie had sent me over the years. All I could think of was what must have been a middle-aged man wearing the big, ugly sunglasses and a baseball hat. Did he look like Tom? Maybe—possibly, possibly not at all. Did I have any of those clippings still? No, I didn't think so. They'd sit on my kitchen counter for a few weeks and then into the garbage they'd go.

I can picture myself that day, kicking up dust as I walked, probably stomped, among the sagebrush. I was frantic and terrified and confused and, at the same time, I think I was tantalized, too.

It wasn't the clear air or the solitude or the famed wide-open spaces of the West that eventually calmed me and slowed my thoughts. No, it wasn't any of that at all. It was simply the effect of time, a small slice of time to adjust to a frightening and thrilling possibility.

I must have breathed deeply while my mind began to allow for fuller thoughts and a more careful review of what I had read and of what Joanie and I had talked about over the years.

Whitey Bulger. James Bulger. Jim or Jimmy to his friends. Whitey on the street, Whitey to the police, and Whitey to all those who follow his tantalizing story in the Boston papers. He was a loan shark. He fixed races at Suffolk Downs and racetracks up and down the Eastern Seaboard. He collected money from anyone doing anything illegal in South Boston, Quincy, or Braintree. Anyone dealing drugs, anyone hijacking trucks, anyone doing anything illegal had to pay Whitey Bulger regularly for the privilege of doing business on his turf. As I remembered it, if you didn't pay, there were two warnings from Whitey. The third warning was no warning at all; it was a bullet in the head. If you owned a legitimate business and Whitey wanted that business, he just might come and take it. He did just that to a young couple, I didn't remember their names, who opened a liquor store on a rotary in South Boston. Whitey wanted the building and the package store as a front for his underworld activities. So he and his men told the wife, who was working the register that particular evening, to get out of the building because it was going to be bombed. When she arrived at home, obviously shaken, there was Whitey and his associate meeting with her husband. Their little daughter, in her pajamas, sat on the associate's lap. Whitey opened and closed the blade of his pocketknife as he spoke. A shiny gun in the little girl's hand and a bag of cash sealed the deal. That was it. The liquor store the young couple had busted their tails to open was Whitey's.

He lived with his mother for as long as she lived and drove an old American-made car. Joanie said once that somewhere in a garage, he kept a Jaguar. But he never drove it around the neighborhood, or Boston for that matter, not wanting to draw attention to himself.

I remembered the *Boston Globe* estimated Whitey Bulger had made somewhere around twenty-five million dollars.

I stopped walking for a moment. Holding the top rail of a rickety fence, I leaned forward and rested my forehead on the backs of my stiff hands and kicked the dirt with the toe of my sneaker, again and again.

What else? What else?

Whitey was an informant. He had been jumping the fence for years helping the FBI to bring down the Italian Mafia, in the North End. Whitey Bulger was a rat—the lowest of the low—even among criminals and especially among the Irish. But when the indictment came down for his arrest, Whitey was gone. He was protected; charmed, some thought. His FBI friends, crooks, too, let him know what was coming and he disappeared. Just gone. Now he's on the FBI's Ten Most Wanted List—wanted for so many things—extortion, racketeering, narcotics, conspiracy, and eighteen murders! And yet the question "Where's Whitey?" is almost a joke in Boston. I mean even Joanie and I joke about her dating him! We should all want him to be caught, of course, but I think the majority of people are somehow rooting for Whitey.

Besides the liquor store, what else had he done specifically? I couldn't quite remember. Then something I read once came to me. It was on the backside of an article my mother sent a long time ago about a new restaurant in Hingham opened by a classmate of mine. There was a piece on the back that wasn't complete because Mother's scissors cut right through it, but I got the idea. A young man, a competitor of Whitey's of some kind, was coming out of his son's birthday party. As he put the key in the ignition, a single man came running from the side of the car and opened fire with a machine gun. The gunman ran away and sped off in a waiting getaway car. The rumor was that the murder was the work of Whitey Bulger. Somewhere in that newspaper story there was also something about the murder, like maybe it was done as some kind of retribution for the nose that was literally bitten right off the face of a man.

I paced up and down the fence line again.

"Now let's think about Tom for a minute," I said to myself. "Tom is from Ohio, so he says. But he's never seen a silver poplar tree. Tom is interested in history and books, but lots of people are interested in history and books, not just Whitey Bulger. Look at the *New York Times* best-seller list, for God's sake. Tom is here because he lost his wife and son and business and has always wanted to see the country. Tom just happens to like dogs. Tom probably pronounced the word 'yesterday' like he was from Massachusetts just by chance. He hasn't been covering an accent. He wears the hats and sunglasses because it's bright and hot here. Hayden is a place anyone would want to be, not just a place where he wouldn't be recognized and no one ever asks a single question."

I stopped and leaned against the fence again. I wasn't convincing myself.

You must believe Tom is who he says he is, I thought. Don't do this to yourself. Too bad if you're the only one within hundreds of miles of here who might know who he really is if he happens to be Whitey. It's not your problem. Oh God! The book. The goddamned book. He's coming here tomorrow to pick up the book. Just get out. Leave it on the porch. Don't talk to him. Don't ask questions and stay away from him, even if he was your chance for a real friend. Don't be curious, just forget it.

"Mummy!" Clara was standing in the back door yelling. "Mummy, Daddy's on the phone!"

Panic welled up inside me again. I shut my eyes and covered them with my hands. George! God, I couldn't talk to him! Should I tell him? No, I can't. He wouldn't understand. I can't talk to him, I thought.

I pulled my hands from my face and yelled to Clara, "Tell him I'll call him later?" The words weren't all the way out of my mouth before I knew what a stupid thing that was to say. I'd never get him at his motel, unless he was asleep.

What was I doing? Why would I put off the man I loved and missed? What was wrong with me? I spun around and faced the bare hill behind the barn and squeezed my eyes closed tight. I felt like crying.

Clara was back on the porch. "He says it's important. Just come to the phone, Mummy!"

Clara watched every step I made across the dry grass, but she didn't say a word, not even as I stepped past her on the porch. I gave her a weak smile, but she responded not at all.

George's voice was ecstatic. "You're not going to believe what we found today!"

"What?" I tried to sound excited.

"We were working over by what would have been the bank of Fossil Lake and one of the students from Kansas State found a complete skeleton of a bat."

"A bat?" I knew there were crocodiles and tiny little horses, but I hadn't pictured bats in the Eocene epoch.

"It is the whole thing! You can see the cartilage and even the wing membranes! It's unbelievable. Whatever it ate last is still in its belly!"

"Oh my God," I said, closing my eyes and rubbing my forehead, trying hard to concentrate on what he was saying.

"I mean you can't imagine what we'll learn from that about the plants and algae, everything—bat behavior even." George was almost breathless. "It's possible this is the oldest bat fossil ever found!"

"Sweetie, that is fabulous." I was genuinely happy for him and my heart was pounding, but not about his wonderful news. It was hard to sound like my normal self, even though I didn't really know how my normal self sounded. Clara stood in the doorway listening.

"Oh, I miss you two," George said, but he sounded too excited to really be missing us.

"We miss you, too," I said. "It won't be much longer now." I clenched my teeth and quietly took a long breath.

"No. We're getting close, just a week more." His voice was calmer. "What's new there?"

"Nothing, really." Oh, how I tried to sound nonchalant, but it was impossible. "You know what, sweetie, I was right in the middle of something in the barn. I hate to do this, but I really have to go."

"I'm sorry!" And he genuinely was. "I go on and on. I should have asked." Oh God. How could he be so nice when I was so crazy? It only made me feel worse.

"That's OK," I said. "But I better go."

"All right. I love you," he said.

"Me, too. Congratulations!" I was relieved to have made it through the conversation.

"Thanks," he said.

I hung up the phone wondering if batteries can recover because the phone didn't beep once.

And there was Clara, staring at me with the worst expression I'd ever seen.

"You're mean!" she yelled. "You lied to Daddy! Why did you tell him you were in the middle of something? You're not!"

Damn it! I was blowing everything. I rubbed my forehead hard with the fingers of my left hand. I had to be calm.

"Oh, honey," I started, but Clara wasn't about to listen to me.

"You're not in the middle of ANYTHING! All you were doing was walking back and forth talking to yourself! You LIED to Daddy!"

She stormed across the kitchen fast, stomping the heels of her tiny brown and white cowboy boots on the tired linoleum.

What an idiot I was.

I found Clara facedown on her unmade bed with her little fists clenched up by her ears. I sat on the edge of the mattress, and she dug her face deeper into the pillow. I put my hand on her back. Her T-shirt was damp with sweat. I said, "I'm sorry, Clara. You *are* right. I didn't tell Daddy the truth."

I thought I saw her fists relax ever so slightly.

"I wasn't really in the middle of something. It's just that I don't feel good." I took a deep breath. "I don't know what it is, but I'll be OK. I just don't feel right today."

She rolled over to study my face. I could tell she was trying to determine if I was being truthful.

"I think I said I was in the middle of something because I didn't want Daddy to worry about me and I thought if I kept talking he'd be able to tell I didn't feel right."

As I spoke I wondered if I was telling her the truth. I decided I was.

"It's just that Daddy loves us so much and he's so happy about his work that I didn't want to ruin it for him just because I feel a little funny."

There was a long silence, and I decided I'd try not to say another word about it. I pushed the hair out of her eyes and couldn't help but say, "You have a beautiful forehead."

She smiled. Then after a bit she said quietly, "Daddy said he can't wait for my birthday."

"He did?" I smiled.

She nodded.

"Well, I sure can wait!" I said. "I don't want you to get a single day older! NOT EVER!"

She reached up to hug me and almost giggled, but not quite.

For Clara, the storm had passed. And for her sake, I guess it had for me, too—at least for a little while.

chapter 21

As she often does when George is away, Clara slept in my bed with me that night.

I read to keep my mind occupied and easily fell asleep, but sometime before one in the morning I woke up in a sweat. I'd like to say "a cold sweat," because that sounds better, but in the heat of our bedroom under the eaves, the sweat had to have been hot.

I think my eyes must have flown wide open in fear. Everything is more worrisome, more ominous, and scarier in the night. I must have been like Robinson Crusoe the night after he saw the footprint on the beach, "fear of danger is ten thousand times more terrifying than danger itself when apparent to the eyes; and we find the burden of anxiety greater, by much, than the evil which we are anxious about."

George is away a lot, and aside from fears about Clara's health, afraid is something I had really been only one other time that I can remember. There was a murderer who was killing women in their homes. The only link they had was that they were all women who lived in towns along railroad routes. Hayden is on a railroad route, and one night, in the middle of the night, I got it in my head that the murderer would ride the trains to Hayden. My fear wasn't swayed at all by the fact that all the killings had taken place a thousand miles away in Texas and New Mexico. That night, in my mind, the murderer was on his way to Hayden and to my house. I only fell asleep when I had 911 speed-dialed into the phone and a baseball bat under the covers next to me.

My nocturnal fears this time were obviously about Tom. In fact, in my darkened bedroom that night, there wasn't a doubt in my mind: Tom Baxter was Whitey Bulger. Try as I might, I couldn't remember any of the reasons I had earlier in the day to disprove the theory.

I leaped from bed and started closing and locking all the windows upstairs, an odd thing to do in the summer, but crazy in Hayden. I sat Clara up and gave her corn-starch juice even though it was a bit early because I was worried that if something happened to me she wouldn't get it at all that night. She drank it without even really waking up. Then I headed down the stairs, assuring myself that if Whitey came after me that night, Clara would be safest upstairs.

With the windows and doors locked, I decided not to

turn on any lights in case he was there outside watching the house. I wouldn't want him to see that I was awake and surmise that I was on to him.

Logical thinking was out the door.

I ran through all I knew about each man, Tom and Whitey, again several times and came up with nothing new. I suppose that's another characteristic of nighttime thoughts: They tend to run in ever repeating circles.

Then I switched gears to decide what I was going to do.

I could go to the police or the FBI with my suspicions. I might get a reward and be able to get a new washer and dryer, and paint the house and buy a new vehicle. I also might get killed if Tom, or Whitey, found out what I had done and was faster than the authorities.

And what if I was wrong and he was just good old Tom Baxter? I'd never forgive myself for such disloyalty. Not to mention the embarrassment of exposing my thinking, which could have possibly been delusional. And poor Lorraine, I couldn't do that to her.

No. I'd have to handle this myself. I just didn't know how.

There's a tradition from the Old West of taking the law into your own hands, a code of vigilantism. Just recently there was the welder in Hayden who earlier in the summer had had just about enough. I read about it in the

Hayden Press, but I like the way I imagined the details even better. A man in his early thirties, I'll call him Robert, worked at a machine shop up on the access road by the interstate. He was putting in a lot of overtime. Coal bed methane brought extra work to the shop, and Robert's boss liked him best, so he was always offered the overtime. Robert had a pretty wife and two kids, a nice clean modular house, a big garage of his own with storage above (he hoped to turn it into an apartment someday for his wife's mother), a fancy truck, and a camper. He and the family liked to spend summer weekends in the camper either at the reservoir or at NASCAR races all over Wyoming and South Dakota. They even went down to Colorado sometimes. Obviously, Robert could use the extra money from time-and-a-half pay.

On a bare hill just east of his property, a methane well was drilled and compressor pump installed. Methane is a clean gas, and the pumps aren't overly intrusive visually, but they pump day and night and never, ever stop making a racket. It sounds like a jet taking off. Robert tried to complain about the pump a number of times to the wildcatlike company that had put it in, but it didn't do any good—they never answered their phones. So one hot Sunday afternoon after a sixty-three-hour workweek, Robert wanted to take a nap. His wife had taken the kids to Wal-Mart and then the movies, so he had a good three hours to himself to sleep. Robert was bone-tired. He stripped down to his underwear, lay down on top of a lavender bedspread, and closed his eyes. But he couldn't sleep. The goddamned pump was too loud.

So Robert stood up. He reached into the top drawer of his dresser, felt for the back left corner, and put his hand right on a key. He walked past the table with his wife's candles and potpourri and unlocked the gun case. He stared at the guns and chose the .30-06 rifle. Then Robert walked out the back door and steadily, not slowly but not quickly, either, just steadily, walked across his Turf Builder Plus green lawn, parted the barbed wire at the edge of his property, and ducked carefully through. He continued at the same pace across the open field—all this with the rifle over his bare shoulder and dressed only in Clorox-bright tighty whities. When he got in range of the pump station, Robert opened fire. And he kept shooting until the goddamned thing shut up!

He walked home the same way he had come and laid himself down for a beautiful, quiet nap.

I'd been watching the paper, but hadn't seen anything lately about Robert's court date.

But how in this situation with Tom could I do anything myself? I wondered. I didn't want to, but maybe I'd have to get George involved. Even my mild-mannered George had the ability to act if he needed to.

When Clara was a tiny baby a whole side of George came out that I had never seen before. We hadn't yet moved into this house, but the incident I remembered definitely cemented our determination to live out in the country, rather than within the city limits of Hayden. We were renting a house on Aberdeen. It was one story, made out of some kind of composite material that actually looked like cardboard under the white paint. It must have been in early to mid-August because Clara was brand-new, just home from the hospital.

All summer long in Hayden while the town peacefully sleeps, on Tuesday and Thursday nights from midnight until two or three in the morning, a truck drives slowly up and down the streets. On Tuesdays it covers neighborhoods east of the train tracks, and on Thursdays, west of the tracks. From an enormous tank in the bed of the truck, gallons and gallons of chemicals are sprayed into the air, onto the lawns, onto the houses, and over the parks, all to control mosquitoes. The chemical is malathion, and there is no medical reason for the spraying, no high incidence of equine encephalitis or anything else like that. Nope, the whole town was doused, and still is, twice a week all summer long, so everyone can enjoy barbecuing in the backyard at any time without those annoying mosquitoes. When I called city hall to complain the first time, I said I was calling about the mosquito spraying. The voice on the other end said, "Oh, I know. We've been gettin' so many calls about it. Geez, they're just terrible this year. Musta been the wet spring. Don't worry, honey, the mayor says he'll up the spraying next week and for the rest of the summer."

I wanted to burn down city hall, but George, my good, good George, found out that there was a group of people who were against the spraying. He went to one of their meetings and even joined a "task force." They did research, and came up with alternatives and plans and all things you're supposed to do. It was a small group, but many were experienced environmental activists who fought for water conservation and opposed the methane drilling. They were good people, trying to do the right thing. But, by the time Clara was born, they hadn't stopped the spraying. They had only gotten so far as to set up a system by which residents could call the town hall to be put on a list of those who didn't want to be sprayed, and if you were on that list and left your porch light on all night, then the driver of the truck would supposedly turn off the sprayer in front of your house.

Thursday nights were our nights to be sprayed on Aberdeen, and in our usual fashion, nearly every Thursday we'd go to bed forgetting it was the night. We'd be so hot and so looking forward to the cool of the evening, we'd throw the windows wide open, put fans on the sills, and go to bed. Then, sometime after midnight, we'd hear the truck coming and smell the sick-sweet smell of malathion, and George and I would each leap from bed, swearing profusely, running from window to window slamming them shut. It was as if our little house were in a cloud of sugar-laced Raid.

I think Clara had been home just a few days and George and I were as exhausted and confused as any new parents. The cradle was arranged sweetly and we did everything the doctors told us to do to give her a healthy start. I was up nursing the baby in our little living room when I heard the rumble of the spray truck in the distance.

"George!" I called in a loud whisper, so as not to shock the baby.

"George!" The truck was getting closer.

"George!" I could smell the malathion. It was overpowering.

I jumped up, nightgown wide open, flicked the porch light on fast. "George!" I was yelling by then. "The *mosquito truck*! The damned mosquito truck!"

"Goddamn it!" George yelled as he ran from the bedroom.

He ran right past me and the by-then-crying infant. He was out on the front porch, and next thing I knew he was smack in the middle of the street, jumping up and down, barefoot, waving his arms and yelling, "Stop! Stop that fucking thing!"

The truck was approaching fast, enveloped in a cloud of spray. There wasn't a hint of it slowing down.

George got out of the way just before he was hit. He ran to our porch and grabbed a brick. He glared at the truck, hesitated for an instant, and then, with his perfect high school quarterback throw, he hurled the brick at the spray truck. There was a loud clank when it hit the tank, but the truck and its chemical shower didn't slow down at all.

The next morning our phone rang, early. It was the mayor of Hayden, who also happened to be George's coach when he was in Little Guy Football some thirty years before.

The mayor said, "George Colter, please don't tell me you're 'the kid' who threw the brick at the mosquito truck last night?"

"Yes, sir," George answered. "That was me."

"Christ, George, why did you have to go and do that?"

"Mr. Nelson, the goddamned driver is supposed to turn the sprayer off in front of our house and he didn't stop the damned thing for an instant. We've got a brand-new baby here and I don't want her exposed to that crap!"

"Sorry to do this, George, but I got to send a cop over

there. Don't go anywhere. I wish you wouldn'a done this."

A nice-looking, black-haired policeman came to the door and I answered, holding Clara all wrapped up in a light cotton blanket.

He looked down at his shiny black shoes. "Is your husband here?"

"Yes, just a minute," I answered.

George came out from the kitchen. He was unshaven, and his hair looked like Lyle Lovett. If I didn't know him, I might have thought he was nuts. I didn't think that was a good sign as he went to talk to the police.

I sat in a chair thinking, I can't believe I'm here with my new baby and the police have come for my husband.

He stepped out onto the porch.

"Hello, Officer." George was a complete gentleman.

"Mr. Colter, I'm here because of an incident that happened last night."

"Yes, sir. I know." George paused. "Aren't you Mike Wilson? Geology one-oh-one about five years ago?"

"Yes! I am. I didn't think you'd remember," the policeman said.

"I remember you well. You had good questions," George said.

"That was a great class!" said the policeman. "Best one I took, by far."

"So you're in the police force now," George said.

"Yup. Went right from Hayden College to the Academy."

They were off talking about that for a while. Then George said, "You know, about that brick, we have a new baby and the driver was dousing our house and I guess I just lost my head."

Officer Wilson was holding the infamous brick in his hand. He looked down at it. "You know, I probably would have done the same thing. But the driver said you almost hit his girlfriend." He looked up at George. "She was riding with him last night and the passenger side window was down."

It seemed to me that both George and the policeman concealed smiles, probably both imagining the driver and his girlfriend on the romantic three-hour spray ride.

"Just don't do it again," the officer said.

George nodded.

Officer Wilson turned to walk down the steps, then he looked back at George.

"Do you want your brick back?"

"Yeah," said George. "I really would. Whenever I have to send a FedEx from home I use it to keep the envelope from blowing away. Thanks."

And that was that. George didn't throw the brick again. He stopped going to the Mosquito Spraying Task

Force meetings. We moved out of town, to Bear Creek Road, as fast as we could.

Walking around the house in the dark that night last summer, with Clara sleeping upstairs, I didn't come up with much except that I'd wait for George. I had no real plan, no new solution, just fear and locked windows and doors.

Before heading back upstairs to my bed and Clara, I remembered there were a few daylight windows in the basement, so I went down to lock those, as well. Percy followed me, as usual never taking his eyes off me, and his presence did give me a bit of comfort, because like any paranoid person worth her salt, I was afraid someone could be hiding down there. The stairs to the basement descend out of the kitchen and they are cement, wider and more inviting than most. I cringed at the grit grinding beneath my feet and realized it would only get worse the farther down I went, and especially in George's shop. I shouldn't go down there barefoot and by the light of a flashlight, I knew, but protecting myself and Clara from a murderer was more important than worrying about being barefoot in the wrong places.

With some effort I was able to get the two windows that were open closed and locked. I turned around and shined the flashlight around the room. There were

George's books, glass cases of fossils and arrowheads, and a big empty spot where he stores equipment when he's home. Oh, how I wished he were home! I just wanted him there so he'd know without me explaining.

Through the open door to the shop I could see a piece of furniture under an old blanket—Clara's new desk. What a father—he'd been working on it for months. All I'd done for her birthday so far was to order a couple of things from a catalog and buy an awful Barbie at Wal-Mart.

I heard the distant, lonely whistle of a coal train headed east. I went back upstairs with a baseball bat in my hand.

chapter 22

The phone rang early the next morning. I knew it would be Joanie.

Without any kind of hello she started right in.

"You know what I hate?"

"Let's see...." I said, looking out the back window at the soft glow of morning light on the sagebrush.

"TV. People live for it. Everything is about the frickin' TV—who's on, and what's on. The newspapers are all about what's on, what was on last night, what will be on tonight. The radio—they'll talk all morning about TV. Magazines. Everything! People on the elevator every single morning—all day, really—talking about what they saw last night. The goddamned secretaries act like the people they see on TV are their best friends! Jesus. I can't stand it!"

"Really?" I said. "This is so shocking," I kidded.

"I can guarantee it's the same out there; you just don't talk to anybody, so you don't know. It's sick. Everyone wants to get home faster and have more time for their precious TV watching."

I thought of Lorraine sending the cross-stitch baby to Rockefeller Center to the TV woman who was having the baby named Jordan.

"The Constitution should have said, 'Life, liberty, and the pursuit of TV time,'" Joanie said.

"The Declaration of Independence," I said.

"What?" Joanie said.

"You mean the Declaration of Independence, not the Constitution," I said.

"Oh yeah, that, too! You're right. I must be watching too much TV! I'm turning into an idiot," she said. "The goddamned thing is on everywhere—restaurants, waiting rooms, airports, everywhere! It's even on at the gym."

"What did you say?" I asked. There was silence. "Did you say 'the gym'?" I asked.

"Yeeeesss." She pretended to sound resigned. "I joined a gym. I had to. I've got to do something about these thick legs."

"Good for you," I said.

"No! Not good for me. Jesus, it's a HUGE waste of time. All it means is that I run, going nowhere on a stupid treadmill, and watch CNN. It's pathetic. Then in the locker room I get to see women who don't hesitate for an instant to walk all over the place stark naked, talking loudly about deodorant and their marvelous weekend plans, even on a Tuesday." Joanie took a sip of coffee. "I can hardly get out of bed in the morning for fear I'll go in there one day and there before me will be Swivel Elf in all her nude glory."

"There is something seriously wrong with you!" I laughed. "Well, tell me this. Are the 'thick legs' any better?"

"God, no!"

"Anything in the news I should know about?" I asked.

"Red Sox lost. I know how you care about that," she said sarcastically. "Ummmm, the *Globe* has been following an ATF agent who uses his government car to go grocery shopping and pick up dry cleaning for his wife. No, nothing really."

"Good," I said. "I'm too hot to take any real news anyway."

"Soooo, how's the, ahhhh"—she made a loud pretend yawn—"grass growing out there? Oh, sorry." Another yawn. "What did you say?" Yawn. "I didn't hear you."

"You've got the picture," I said. If only she knew.

"Well, I better go," Joanie said. "Swiv's here. Gotta get back to work."

There. That was done. For some reason I just wasn't ready to tell Joanie about Tom. Not yet. And somehow I was relieved.

chapter 23

When Tom came for the book, how would I act? He knew my license plate number and what books I had on my shelf, so surely he'd be able to tell I was on to him. Maybe I should take Clara and leave the house and just put the book on the front porch. But where would I go? And with my luck, I'd stay away all day and he'd show up right when I got home, whenever that was.

Clara sat up at the kitchen counter eating her cereal, and we talked about her birthday party. My mouth was moving and I answered her questions, but my mind was mostly on myself and how I would handle seeing Tom.

"Can I just have a party with grown-ups?" Clara asked.

"Just grown-ups?" Leave it to an only child to want that.

"Yes. I hated my birthday last year."

"You did?" For God's sake, we had all those kids over!

I thought it was what she wanted. After all that and she hated it?

"'Member?" She looked exasperated. "Jessie hogged all the candy and tried to pop the balloons. She can be a pain in the you-know-what." Clara took a bite of cereal. "I didn't get any of the good prizes, either."

"Oh, right." No. I didn't really remember any of that.

"So, I just want grown-ups this year." She started counting on her fingers. "Me, you, Daddy, Grammy, Casey." She was out of fingers on her right hand. "That's it."

"OK." I pictured Casey tying a black paper blindfold on Lorraine's head, then spinning her around for pin-the-tail-on-the-donkey.

"And Mummy, I do not want that cake with whipped cream and strawberries!"

"OK." I made an angel food cake last year from scratch. It took a dozen egg whites. Apparently it wasn't a hit.

"I just want a regular cake with pink and white frosting," Clara said.

"OK."

"Mummy, a REGULAR cake." She could tell I was thinking about something else. "Or an ice cream cake, but it has to be pink and white."

"All right. I'll get right on it!" I smiled at her and she smiled the cutest smile right back.

I brought her cereal bowl to the sink and then spun around fast.

"What, Mummy?" she asked, looking alarmed. "What's wrong?"

"I thought I heard a car door shut," I said, my feet frozen to the spot by the sink.

Clara jumped from the stool and ran to the window.

"You did!" She scrambled for the front door, yelling, "It's Grammy and Mr. Baxter!"

Oh God! This early? At least Lorraine was with him.

I went out on the front porch. Clara was already by the car with Lorraine, talking about the birthday party, I'm sure. And there he was coming up the steps in his tight Wranglers and cowboy boots. He wore the cowboy hat and sunglasses, too, of course. My heart pounded and I was most definitely afraid—afraid of Tom, afraid of Whitey, afraid of what I didn't know, afraid of the future, and afraid of myself.

Then he smiled at me, bright and warm and old. I tried hard to determine if there was anything in the face that would show for certain that he was Whitey Bulger. If it was there I didn't see it. In twenty-four hours he hadn't changed a bit, I realized. Everything that I liked about him was right there in front of me still. I was the one who was different. Suspicion had changed me.

I held the book out to him. Lorraine waved from the

car. "Hi, honey!" she yelled across the yard. "Tom's ta-kin' me down to see Fort Johnson. He just can't believe I haven't been there since 1960, I bet."

Fort Johnson, the site of a lesser-known Indian attack, is only sixty-five miles from Hayden.

Tom took the biography from me and said, "Thanks so much. I can't wait to start this." Then he turned to-ward Lorraine and playfully said in a loud voice, "She's turning that damned television off." He raised the book in the air. "We're going to read to each other instead!"

Lorraine shouted happily, "He thinks he's going to get me all straightened out!" Her black hair was shiny and she looked younger than her years.

"For God's sake, she thinks those people on the *To-day* show are her friends!" he teased.

That reminded Lorraine of something. "Oh, honey, I forgot to tell you, I got the most beautiful thank-you note in the mail from Marlena Adams herself. She just loved the present I sent for Jordan. Can you believe it!"

"No I can't," I said. "That's incredible!"

Tom went back down by the car. He looked up at me on the porch and thanked me again.

I was almost through it. He'd be gone in a minute.

He handed the book through the passenger side win-dow to Lorraine, then looked up and said to no one in particular, "Isn't that a gorgeous tree?"

"No it is not!" Lorraine exclaimed. "Those things are trash! Suckers everywhere." She shook her head. "I can't believe you like that tree."

"It's beautiful," he said, still looking up in the air.

From the top step of the porch I said, "Didn't you ever see a tree like that in Ohio, Tom?" The words were out of my mouth before I could stop myself. "I bet they grow there, too."

Even under his sunglasses I could tell his eyebrows were raised. "Nope, never did, Madam Arborist." He tipped his hat and started around the back of the car to the driver's side.

"Stay cool today, Kate," he said calmly. Completely relaxed was his expression.

On the far side of the car, through the back windows I saw him reach out for a stringy columbine. The blossom disappeared in his fist.

chapter 24

Inside the house I went straight to work.

When Joanie was joking a few weeks before about picking up with Whitey, she said she was his type. I think she said he likes blond and buxom. Lorraine's buxom, but not blond.

I called Joanie. She picked up after a few rings and said, "I'm on the other line. Call you right back."

"Wait! Just one question," I said quickly. "Did you say Whitey likes blonds or brunettes?"

"Blonds." The phone clicked off; Joanie was back to business.

I scanned the bookshelves in the living room and in our bedroom for tree guides. No luck. I ran to the basement, slowing down when I passed Clara, who was by then coloring at the dining room table. George had Peterson's guides to everything, birds, shells, fossils—but no trees.

In a back corner of the basement I remembered I had

a box with old letters. Maybe there was something in there with a picture of Whitey. For the first time in my life, I opened an old box like that, chock-full of my past, and I wasn't even slightly distracted by all the unexpected memories it brought to the fore. I flipped quickly past letters handwritten by my dead father and didn't pause for a second at pictures of myself with no gray in my hair and not a wrinkle in sight. No. I was on a mission for clippings of any kind. No luck there, either.

I marched upstairs and grabbed my wallet.

"C'mon, Clara. We're going to the library."

The Hayden Public Library sits shaded under enormous old cottonwoods. When we pulled into the parking lot, there, spread throughout the canopy of one of the cottonwoods, were maybe twenty hulking dark figures. Turkey vultures. They looked too big for the dwindling branches that held them. I've seen them in the trees in town a hundred times, but still their heft and stillness are always eerie.

Clara went happily to the children's room with its books and wide selection of videos and toys.

I found *Peterson's Field Guide to North American Trees*. Poplar. *Populus*. Silver poplar. White poplar. The description of white poplars sounded very close to what we call silver poplars, and the guide showed none in New England and just a very light smattering of them in Ohio.

So what did that tell me? Exactly nothing. It's possible Tom might never have seen one in Ohio.

I went to the reference desk. The keg-shaped librarian had her back to me as she leaned on the doorjamb that led to the back room. She was talking loudly and slowly about her ten-year-old cocker spaniel and his ear troubles.

"Vet says that back east, cockers get maggots in their ears—swarms of 'em snug under those big, droopy earflaps. Must be all that humidity they have back there," she said to someone in the back room whom I could neither hear nor see.

My stomach lurched and I cleared my throat.

The librarian turned around slowly.

"Oh! Hi, hon. I didn't see you there." She shuffled to the counter between us. "What can I do for ya today?"

"I'm wondering how I might be able to see old copies of the *Boston Globe*."

"Oh geez, hon. I don't know." She lowered herself into a chair by a big computer terminal. "But let me see.... They say all this is going to be computerized someday."

What good does that do me now? I thought.

She stared at the computer awhile, then hoisted herself up and made her way to the back room. After a few minutes she returned with a pen and a piece of paper.

"Alice, the director of the library, is at a dentist appointment. I'll need to get with her on this and call you back this afternoon. Let me have your name and number, hon."

There was a time when I knew the Hayden librarians, but that time had passed. Nothing like getting information in a hurry! I gave her my phone number, collected Clara, and we left.

That afternoon there was a message on my machine. The voice was loud and deliberate. "This message is for Kate Colter. This is Charlene Long at the reference desk in to the library. We can order the *Boston Globe* for you on microfilm. I would just need the dates yer lookin' for and we can have those here in about two weeks. Now, you won't be able to take them from the library, but you can use the microfilm reader in Alice's office. You could look at it here at the library for two weeks before we'd have to send it on back. Please call me back and I'll get to fillin' out the inter-library loan form."

Two weeks! That was an eternity, but I called Charlene to get the process going. And it's not like I could just hop in the car and drive to another town to a better library like you can elsewhere. Denver would probably be my best bet, and that's a good seven hours away. Plus, who knew, maybe I wouldn't even see Tom for another two weeks.

I caught Charlene just before the library closed.

"Oh. Sure. OK. Let's see...." Her talk was so leisurely I wanted to explode, but I didn't.

"Let me just ask you a few questions and then I'll get this off tomorrow."

She got my name and address and spoke as she filled in each line on her form, drawing out the words to keep in step with her handwriting: "Kate ... Colter ... 12 ... Bear ... Creek ..." and so on.

Just as she finished and I was about to hang up the phone, good old Charlene threw me a corker. "I'll call you when this comes in," she explained. "Funny thing happened today, somebody else was askin' 'bout the *Boston Globe*. Small world."

"What? The *Globe*?" I'm sure I shouted. "Who was it?"

"Oh, I don't know his name. Some man."

"What did he look like?"

"Oh, he was older," she said.

"Describe him, please!" My frustration mounted.

"I don't know, just a regular older man."

Jesus! Couldn't she think of anything? What is wrong with people?

"Anyway, he didn't want the microfilm; he was just wonderin' about the computer—could you see it on the computer yet. And you know, they say that's comin' for a lot of newspapers, but not yet."

"Did you tell him about me?"

"Oh geez. I don't know, hon." Her pace was not increasing with mine and she was so obtuse, it must not have occurred to her to be defensive. "Maybe in passing."

She definitely told him, I thought.

She said, "If I did, he must not a' been too interested 'cause when I told him it wasn't on the computer, he left pretty quick."

chapter 25

The next morning Clara and I came home from picking up the checkbook and ledger from Mr. Stanley's office, and stuck between the screen door and the frame was a piece of paper. It looked like a receipt of some kind, but when I pulled it out I saw the handwriting.

Kate—

If you can, please meet me at The Bronco this afternoon at two. No need to try to reach me before then. Just
come if you can. I'll be there either way.

Tom

chapter 26

Obviously, I was scared. But I was excited, too. I couldn't help it. The Bronco was a public place, how dangerous could that be?

It was as if nothing else were affecting me, but my anxiety about Tom. I don't remember any more conversations with Joanie. I don't remember how, or if, I slept at night. I can't say what Clara was doing because I'm not sure. The pony, Timmy, by that time was doing much better, but his improvement really gave me no pleasure. I can't even remember if I called the Nicholsons to report on his progress. I do remember that the washing machine broke, as I predicted it would, right in the middle of the wash cycle with a whole load of clothes floating in soapy water. I didn't swear. I didn't complain. I just rinsed everything in the kitchen sink, hung it out to dry, and emptied the machine by the bucketful, pouring gray water onto hard dust behind our house.

In hindsight, it seems strange how little I thought

of George through all that was going on. And Lorraine hardly crossed my mind. If Tom Baxter were Whitey Bulger, wouldn't she have been in the most danger of all? I didn't worry about that. No, I was too wrapped up in a nervous, tantalized frenzy.

I did worry that Tom's invitation to The Bronco was a trap, that he might lure me to town and then kidnap Clara from our house. So to foil any plan of that kind, I brought Clara and our neighbor Casey to the town pool for a swim. The bag was packed with towels, sunscreen, and extra food and juice, just in case I was gone for a while. I told them not to go anywhere with anyone and I had some errands to do. Casey winked, assuming my plan was to shop for Clara's birthday.

As usual, town was quiet. Heat waves rose off Main Street to the north. I parked and stepped out of the truck onto the hot pavement. No sooner had my head felt the beating sun than I heard, "Yoooo hooooo, Kate!" from across the street.

There was Lorraine's ex-friend Dalene, waving at me from under the awning of the Hallmark store.

"Hi, Dalene," I shouted and kept moving, hoping to show this wasn't a time for a useless chitchat.

"Just getting balloons for Kristi," she said. "She's got a new job up to the hospital."

"That's great." I couldn't remember if Kristi was her

daughter or her daughter-in-law. "Tell her congratulations." I waved again and went on my way, not thinking for a minute how intrigued Dalene might be to see me going into The Bronco in the middle of the afternoon.

Inside the bar it was dark and chilly. I don't usually picture an Old West bar as air-conditioned, but The Bronco was as cold as a walk-in cooler. The walls are covered with shellacked shingles, each scorched with the brands of different Wyoming ranches— L Lazy Y, Z Cross, J Bar 9, and so on, including everyone's favorite, 2 Lazy 2P. The dark glass eyes of tired snowshoe rabbit and rattlesnake mounts peer out from lit cases. The bar itself extends halfway down the right side of the room. At the back are a few tables with benches and a poorly lit pool table with faded green felt. George and I used to come into The Bronco every so often, just to sit at the bar and have a beer, probably trying to get some kind of hometown, Old Westy feeling.

As my eyes adjusted to the dim light, I saw a bear of a woman bartender leaning on her elbows talking with a pale, skinny, much younger woman smoking a cigarette. The skinny one wore a tight aqua tank top and had a tattoo. There was a fat beagle at her feet. At the far end of the bar sat Tom, with his hands around a bottle of beer. He didn't turn to look as I came in.

I took a deep breath, hoping the pounding of my

heart would stop. I carefully climbed up on the stool next to him.

He still didn't look at me. "You came," he said.

"Yup," I answered. "God, it's so hot out! It feels good in here."

He turned to me with a closed-lipped, small smile and asked, "You want a beer?"

I said I did.

He held his hand up to get the bartender's attention. "We'll have another one down here," he said.

She pulled a bottle out, popped off the cap, backed toward us, slid the beer in front of me, and never stopped her conversation with the skinny woman in the tank top.

Tom pulled a bill off a wad of cash and left it on the bar. I thought with a pile of cash like that he must be a criminal.

"Let's go back here," he said, standing up to walk to the back of the bar.

I followed. He waited for me to sit down, then sat down himself. He took off his cowboy hat and put it on the bench next to him. He took off his sunglasses and laid them on the table by the Tabasco sauce against the wall. I was able to see Tom closely and he was handsome. But I just didn't really know what Whitey Bulger looked like.

Tom didn't say anything, at first.

My chest was tight and I'm sure my palms were sweating. I turned to the wall and said something stupid like, "Did you ever think there could be so many brands?"

There was a silence. Then he said, "No I didn't, but I don't want to talk about that."

"OK," I said. Oh God, here it comes!

"I've never heard you talk about your mother," he said.

My mother? What? My mother! I nearly spit the beer out of my mouth.

"Uh, no, I guess you haven't," I sputtered.

"Why is that?" he asked, lifting the beer bottle to his mouth and looking at me out of the corners of his blue eyes.

"I don't know." I really didn't know. "I guess because there's not much to say."

"What do you mean?" he said.

"I don't know. We're just not that close."

He didn't respond, so I kept going. "There's nothing bad, it's just that we don't talk much, or see each other very often. I guess I didn't turn out the way she wanted, but it's not that big of a deal—not much for me to say about it." I stopped.

"You see her much?" he asked.

"No. I haven't been back east for four years. And she wouldn't come out here again."

"You keep in touch with many people back there?"

I decided to say, "No."

He looked down at his beer, and then up at me, and said, "I loved my mother very much."

I nodded.

"In fact, I loved her more than anyone in the world. I loved my mother more than I've ever loved anyone in my life."

I felt dizzy not being able to imagine where this was going.

"You saw me cross myself at the rodeo."

I nodded, but didn't take my eyes off him.

"I do that every day, a few times a day, asking for forgiveness. Forgiveness for what I did to my mother." He stopped and looked down at his fingers, which he'd started tapping on the table.

"Have you noticed anything about me?" he asked.

"What do you mean?"

"Well, this beer for example." He lifted it to his mouth, tipped his head back, and set the bottle back on the table between us.

I shook my head no.

"Didn't notice anything in your barn last week?"

God, no. What was he talking about?

I shook my head again.

"I don't drink," he said.

"What do you mean?"

"I mean what I said. I don't drink," he said sternly.

"You'll have a drink, but you don't drink it?" I asked. "Is that what you're saying?"

"Yes."

"OK," I said. I'd have to take this one step at a time. My heart rate was finally returning to somewhere near normal.

"I don't drink it," he reiterated.

"Then why do you get the beer?"

"Control." His eyes were cold. "It would be too easy to say no. This takes control. To see it, smell it, even taste it just a little bit, but not drink it. And if you say you don't drink, then people want to talk about that. They say"—he scrunched his face up and imitated somebody's high-pitched, annoying voice—"'Oh, you have a drinking problem? My father had a drinking problem ... blah blah blah blah....' Now, who the hell wants to talk about all that every time someone asks if you want a drink?"

"I see what you mean," I said.

"See, right now I'd just wait for you to go to the ladies' room, then order two more beers, hand this one to the bartender, you'd come back, see two cold ones, and never notice." He tipped his bottle again, but there was no swallow. "See?"

"And that day in the barn?" I asked.

"You gave me the beer. When you went to get something, medicine or something, for the horse's leg, I dumped the bottle in the stall."

I waited to see where he would take this.

"You asked me up at the Custer Battlefield that day if I was Catholic."

"Yes," I said.

"And I lied to you."

I looked down at the table. "I know."

"My mother, bless her soul, was Catholic. The church was everything to her. The greatest thing any man could do in her eyes was to devote his life to the church—be a priest. And I loved her more than anything and I wanted to please her and make her proud. I thought I must have loved God and Jesus and the church because she did."

He was rolling along now.

"So I did what the best Irish Catholic sons do—I went into the priesthood. And oh was my mother proud. I could do no wrong. My brothers and sisters were nothing compared with me in her eyes. I was her perfect son. Her own flesh and blood—a man of the cloth. She swished around the neighborhood, to her tea parties and to the corner butcher shop, secure in her success. No matter that her husband spent too much time at the bar, no matter that her firstborn came after only seven and a half months of marriage, no matter that my older brother, her son, left his young wife and two little kids for another woman. None of that mattered anymore for my dear mother; she had a son who was going to be a priest. And it was me."

I listened for a Boston accent, but didn't really hear one. If anything, he almost had a bit of the Irish lilt.

"I was a good altar boy and I did fine at St. John's."

"St. John's in Brighton? Are you originally from Massachusetts?" I jumped in. He is from Boston!

"Yes." His look told me I shouldn't interrupt again— no more questions. "But underneath it was starting to fall apart," he went on. "I didn't know it at first; in fact I didn't know it until it was too late. I was drinking in my room late at night alone. I only knew how much I was drinking when I'd see the empty bottles in the morning. During the day I couldn't keep my eyes off the young mothers who brought their children to catechism. Even the secretaries looked good. I prayed and prayed for it to stop. I thought of my mother and how much I loved her and I just tried to keep my head down.

"Then one morning just before my ordination, over my eggs and toast, I realized I didn't know where I had been the night before. I felt awful. My head pounded, my stomach twisted, and I had only a flicker of a memory of walking down a dark street. I knew I hadn't been alone. But I couldn't remember any more. I just had a sick feeling."

He stopped talking and turned his head to the side. Then looked up at the ceiling. It seemed hard for him to keep going. I waited.

"Well, I had done the unspeakable. And the monsignor knew and I knew God knew. For a man it was human, but for a man about to become an ordained priest, unspeakable. I knew it was over. I knew I could never drink again, either. I broke my dear mother's heart."

He made a fist and gently pounded it on the table.

"And what was the worst part? Years of effort lost? No. Embarrassment? No."

"Your mother," I said.

"Not just my mother, but her face when I told her. The look in her eyes. It was as if all she had worked for her whole life, all that she cared about, all that she loved, all of it was being torn from her. Torn from her. Torn from her by me! 'The Lord giveth and the Lord taketh away,' but it must be even worse when it is given and taken by your own son."

I didn't know what to say. This was so different than anything I had been imagining.

"I always tried to make it up to her. As long as she lived I provided for her and tried to make her life comfortable. I supported her."

"By?" I asked.

"I sent her money. I had to get out; I couldn't face

her disappointment every day, so that's when I went to Ohio. But I sent her money always." He paused. "And I can't help but cross myself when I think of her, which is often."

"Why are you telling *me* this?" I asked.

"Because I lied to you and you knew it," he said. "And because I can tell you're wondering."

"Wondering?"

"Yes. You've been wondering about me. And the way you looked at me yeste'day when I picked up the book." He paused and smiled. "Like you were on to me or something."

"On to you?" I asked, probably with a nervous laugh. Would he mention the library and the *Globe*?

"Yeah, on to me. Well, there you have it. That's the big secret."

"OK." My eyes must have been wide and I shook my head slightly from side to side.

"I like it here and I hope to stay, but Lorraine doesn't know anything about this. You can tell her if you want, but I'd just as soon do it myself when she's ready. She's a good girl, you know."

I said, "I know."

He stood up. The meeting was over. Before I walked out into the sharp light of Main Street, he gave me a look I'll never forget. I didn't understand it, but I won't forget it. It was a strange kind of smile, and I couldn't tell if it meant he trusted me, or he loved me, or maybe he was just pleased with himself because at last he was certain he'd had enough of me. Then he leaned over, kissed my cheek, and with his mouth close to my ear said quietly, "The Bible says, 'Be not curious in unnecessary matters: for more things are shown unto thee than men understand.'"

chapter 27

Sara Wotkyns, my mother's high school classmate, visited us every summer of my childhood. She'd come to see Mother as part of her annual trip "back home." The two old friends would sip iced tea in the cool shade of the maple tree in our backyard, talking to each other in soft, polite voices. Their conversations were about the usual things—husbands, children, and houses. There never seemed to be a rush of any kind to the visits, or any feeling that Sara might have anything else she needed to do that day. She was petite and pretty and sweet. And to me, even as a little girl, Sara Wotkyns was as boring as the day is long. There was nothing interesting about her. Until one year, during her visit, I found out what she could do.

She and Mother were seated primly in the lawn chairs chatting. Mother called me over to hear Sara tell about her daughter, who was excelling at ballroom dancing competitions in Texas. As Sara spoke she nonchalantly looked over the arm of her chair, reached down, and plucked a four-leaf clover!

"Here you go," she said, handing me the lucky charm.

I was flabbergasted, by the fact that she found it, but also by how she didn't seem at all thrilled with the discovery. I'd looked for a four-leaf clover for as long as I could remember, and never once found one.

Sara leaned forward in her chair and said, "Oh, there's another one."

I couldn't believe it. She told us she found them all the time. She could see them without even trying. I didn't know if it was a trick, or a gift, or that it meant she saw the world differently from the rest of us. What I did know was that I certainly saw her differently.

In those few moments, someone who had interested me not at all became extraordinary. She became someone of mysterious ability. My mother had known this woman nearly all her life and never had any idea about the four-leaf clovers. Had we been sitting inside, or on a perfect lawn with no clover, we never would have known about Sara Wotkyns and her exceptional view of the world.

George can see aspects of the world differently from most people. His unusual vision is based on knowledge and experience. And what he knows about all that he sees, opens up for his mind an entire ancient world. It's a world to which most of us, nearly all of us, are completely oblivious. In the sloping striations of sedimentary rocks on the sides of the road, he sees shifting tectonic plates. In a petrified mollusk in the dirt, something I would stomp right on top of with my clumsy sneaker, he sees the ocean that once covered the dusty plains. He'll show you what he finds, but he never shows off what he knows, and rarely does he even elaborate on how a piece he holds in his hand reveals to him a better understanding of what came before us on earth.

George is handsome, modest, quiet, and kind, but what keeps me here, here with him, is his mind. It's a mind that doesn't need talk, or even companionship in its thought, and it's so intently focused on a subject that it cannot stop itself from thinking. The magnet for me is the way George sees what I can't and how he combines knowledge and imagination to understand what the rest of us miss.

When I first came to Wyoming to visit George, he did what every good Western man should do with an Eastern woman. He took me hiking. It was a day late in the fall, almost Thanksgiving, but it felt more like a dry, temperate winter day. My face had to adjust to sharp wind and light. I remember squinting and after a bit having a hard time enunciating, as my lips chilled beyond comfortable. We hiked and hiked, our path weaving among sagebrush and prickly pear. The distant vistas that didn't change as we walked and the absence of trees made me feel strangely as if we weren't really covering ground. The sensation the landscape gave me was odd, but it didn't matter because we were so busy talking. We talked about everything: books, movies, favorite teachers, childhood friends, college friends. We covered old boyfriends and girlfriends, and what went wrong, where they were now. We compared those from the East to those from the West. In a teasing way, George told me for the first time that I asked too many questions. "People around here don't do that. We just don't," I remember him saying. "So you better cool it, or they'll all think I brought back one of those nosy Eastern girls."

He also told me about his father's death. George wasn't there with him when he died, and he was sorry about that. In his eyes I could see regret, certainly, and sadness, too, but also there was a steadiness and sureness. The twenty-nine-year-old George Colter was obviously an adult.

We must have walked for three or four hours, and just as we came up over a knoll near where the car was parked, George stooped to pick something up. He told me to hold out my hand and then placed there what I thought was a rock. It wasn't very big, smaller than my palm, and had a tapering cylindrical shape.

"*Belemnitella*," he said. "Belemnite."

"What?"

"Cretaceous period," he said.

"What are you talking about?" I asked. "What is it? A fossil?"

"This is probably sixty-five to a hundred million years old," he said, tracing his finger along the gray cylinder in my open hand. "It's part of the body of a squid. This was all a great shallow ocean, the Sundance Sea." He looked out over the horizon. "There were dinosaurs on the shores, flying reptiles in the sky, and marine reptiles swimming the sea." He pointed toward the sun lowering on the horizon. "A great volcanic arch to the west of the sea went all the way from Mexico to Canada."

I couldn't believe what I was holding in my hand!

"George! You just found this? Aren't you thrilled?" I gushed.

"Oh sure, it's always incredible to hold the real thing," he said. "But they're all over the place. Just look around."

I turned and looked to my right and then to my left, but I didn't see anything that looked like what I was holding.

"Right there," he said, pointing behind me.

I turned, my sight following an invisible line from the

tip of his finger to the ground. Still I saw nothing but grayish, cracked, alkaline dirt.

George went closer, his pointing finger nearing the ground.

And then I saw it! Five belemnites scattered across the ground!

I was silent for most of the ride back to Lorraine's that day. I just couldn't believe the variety of conversations we'd had. Yet, all the while, George had a hundred-million-year-old world in his head. I thought we were just chatting and walking along, but the whole time he was seeing abundant evidence of that time and those creatures literally right under our feet. I had thought of myself as someone who was observant, inquisitive, and educated, but there I was with George, ignorant, unaware, and oblivious. And he didn't seem to mind.

chapter 28

George would be home soon, very soon, thank God. And I had a decision to make. What would I tell him about Tom? Anything?

After talking with Tom at The Bronco I was calm, for a day or two. Or maybe it was less. I thought that perhaps all my suspicions should be put to rest by what he had told me. He did have Boston connections, which would explain the way he said "yeste'day" at Shipton's. He had real skeletons in his closet. They weren't the bones I had thought they were, but they were bones nonetheless, and their existence may have given me the sense that he was hiding something, or that he wasn't who he appeared to be. The likelihood that Tom Baxter was Whitey Bulger was one in millions, and I was all worked up over a chance thought. More likely than not, the thought was an insane leap of the imagination.

But, after a little while, as my mind sifted through the meeting at the bar, like a miner panning for gold, what fell away was the big story he told, and what was left were smaller things like the way his eyes looked when he said the word "control" and his quote from the Bible at the end: "Be not curious in unnecessary matters: for more things are shown unto thee than men understand."

I wanted it all to stop. I wanted to be done with it one way or another, and especially before George came home. I tried to put the pieces together, but they didn't quite fit.

Tom had the thin scar on his hand and wrist, but I'd never heard or read about Whitey Bulger having a scar like that. I had no indication that Tom took any medicine, never saw a bottle or saw him take a pill, but I remembered that Whitey was on some kind of high-blood-pressure medication. Tom had a wad of green bills, but I hadn't seen the pouch where Whitey supposedly kept his cash and his pearl-handled jackknife. Tom didn't wear Whitey's Alcatraz belt buckle, either.

All I had was a fit man in his sixties who liked history, books, and women; who had a complicated past; who seemed to be in Hayden, Wyoming, for no real reason; someone who made calls at pay phones and always used cash, who was Irish Catholic and originally from Boston. He was charming and he seemed to like dogs. And when he sensed I was getting close to asking personal questions, he headed me off at the pass with a corker of a story that would quiet me down.

It was as if Tom and I were dancing, each of us simultaneously enjoying ourselves and feeling uncomfortable in the peculiar rhythm, both of us savoring the precarious pattern and neither jumping in with the heavy-handed direct questions that hung heavily in the air. It was affection and intrigue held together at a distance by fear and suspicion. It was a dance that could go on and on, until something or someone gave.

chapter 29

Friday, August 4, 1995, the day George was coming home. Clara and I awoke earlier than usual, fed the animals, and started straightening up the house for George's homecoming and for Clara's birthday party the following day.

The phone rang and I ran to pick it up, thinking it would be George.

"Hi, honey." It was Lorraine. "What time does George get home?"

"Morning, Lorraine." I was glad to hear her voice. "I'm not sure. He's got a long drive, so I bet it won't be until tonight."

"Oh, OK," she said. "To tell you the truth, I'm glad. I've just got so much to do today; I don't think I would even have time to get out there after work to see him, let alone on my lunch break. Poor thing, he'll just have to wait to see his mother until the party tomorrow evening." She laughed at her own humor.

"What do you have going on today?" I asked.

"Oh my Lord, honey, I have sooooo much to do. I woke up at five o'clock just thinking about it. It's been hours ago since I've been ready for work. I've already got my hair out of the rollers and I'm just sittin' here working on a cross-stitch—I got the most beautiful seafoam green backing on sale at Coast to Coast."

"Who's this one for?" I was sidetracked by the cross-stitch.

"Oh, I don't know. Just getting ahead, I guess," she said.

"So what all is going on today?" I asked again. I could hear the television in the background.

"Well, you know Betty, at work, is retiring in October …"

Whenever I hear "Betty, at work" I imagine myself calling directory assistance and saying, "Hayden, Wyoming. Betty at Work's home number please."

Lorraine hadn't stopped talking; my mind just wandered for an instant. "… and I'm in charge of the retirement party," she went on. "I already told you, didn't I, that it's out at the Holiday." Holiday Inn. "I wanted the atrium—wouldn't that be gorgeous for a party?—but evidently our group isn't large enough, so we're getting a partial ballroom. So today, I have to check the RSVP list, see who's paid and how much we have so far, and I have to call the company that makes the retirement plaque. Betty doesn't know about the plaque. Of course, I'm supposed to do all that between making appointments, checking in patients, and answering the phone!"

"Does Betty know about the party?" I asked.

"Oh my Lord, yes, honey. I had to get the addresses from her so I could send invitations to her family members. She has a niece coming clear from San Diego for the party. I can't imagine what that would cost, but I guess she hasn't seen Betty for a number of years, and Betty certainly isn't getting any younger. Anyway, I've got to go out to the Holiday on my lunch break because Tami Johnson— Remember her? She used to work for Dr. Frielander before she moved down to Cheyenne. Well, she called the Holiday to make a reservation and they quoted her sixty dollars for the room. She said, 'Now wait a minute, this is for the Mountain Vision retirement party for Betty Bradley, isn't there a special rate?' Would you believe the girl at the Holiday didn't know anything about it! Well, there sure is a special rate. Anyone staying at the motel who's going to Betty's party gets a special rate of fifty dollars. So I'll have to go on out there today to get it straightened out."

"Oh my gosh," I said.

"They'll be setting up for the Holiday Expo, too. So that'll make it fun to go."

"What's the Holiday Expo?" It sounded familiar, but I couldn't remember what it was.

"That's where businesses set up booths with all of their holiday merchandise, and services and whatnot. Oh, they have raffles and door prizes."

"You mean like Christmas stuff? In August?"

"I know, honey, it seems early. But they do it every year. It'll be here before we know it," she reminded me.

"I guess you're right," I said. "How was your time with Tom at Fort Johnson?"

"Oh, it was marvelous," she said.

"Did you walk all around where the fort used to be and down to the creek?"

"Yeeess we did. I got the worst blisters, too. I had on my new tennies. You'd think I'd know better!"

"Doesn't Tom know a lot about history?" I asked.

"You can say that again!" She laughed. "Speaking of Tom, I don't mean to be rude, and I sure hope you don't mind me asking … but is he invited to Clara's birthday party tomorrow?"

"Oh, Lorraine!" I hadn't even thought about Tom at the birthday party, but I'd have to say yes now, since she asked. "Sure, he's invited. I'm sorry. I should have made that clear."

"No, honey, that's fine." She sounded like it really was

fine. "I didn't want to put you on the spot, but I thought you might have just forgotten to mention it."

"Please bring him," I said, thinking how tolerant Lorraine is of me, always. There she is working full-time, with everything all squared away, even ready for work early, and I can't even get it together to organize a little birthday party for a seven-year-old!

"Oh sugar!" she exclaimed as if she were swearing. "I was early and now look, I'll be late for work! We'll see you tomorrow at five."

After Lorraine's call, Clara and I spent most of the day in the barn. Timmy was ready to go home. His pastern was healed beyond needing daily care, and in time he just might be sound. I'd called the Nicholsons to tell them Timmy was ready and they wanted me to bring him out to their ranch the next day because their grandchildren would be there when he arrived. So I had the day all worked out—Clara would go to Casey's house around nine o'clock, to give George and me time to do whatever needed to be done to get ready for the party, then I'd take Timmy to the Nicholsons' and pick up the ice cream cake at the Dairy Queen. If Clara was home from Casey's by then, she and George could have some time together before the party.

Clara wanted to give Timmy a bath so he'd look his

prettiest for the arrival back at the Nicholsons'. It was a good idea and the afternoon was so hot, why not?

I squirted the shampoo and a little old-fashioned laundry bluing (a trick for whitening ponies) in the bucket and then took it to the kitchen for some warm water. It was more for the comfort of our hands than for Timmy. We tied Timmy outside and started first on his left side, wetting him with the hose. Clara ran to the barn for sponges and brushes. She returned with her hands full of the red and blue and green bristles.

"A bath is a good time to wash brushes, right, Mum?"

"Good girl!" I was glad she remembered.

I lathered the pony while she slowly scrubbed the brushes against each other in the warm water. Occasionally she would carry a sudsy, dripping brush or sponge to rub Timmy for a moment, but she was really having more fun with the soapy water in the bucket than with the pony's bath.

I rinsed his left side and started on the right. The cold water from the hose felt good as small droplets bounced from Timmy's hide back at me.

I sprayed and scrubbed, wondered what I should do. How would I act toward Tom at the party? Could I ignore all my questions? Should I go to the FBI? Should I ask Joanie to go to the Boston Public Library to get the *Boston Globe* on microfilm faster? Should I just ask Tom outright? No. I couldn't. I couldn't do any of that. I'd have to rely on George to help me figure it all out.

"OK, honey," I said to Clara. "Time to rinse the brushes."

We pulled them from the bucket and lined them up on the cement slab for rinsing.

"Lie them all on their sides," I said. "That way the soap will run off and the wood won't rot." Then I wondered if wood ever could rot here in the parched West. Clara did as I said. I handed her the hose and she washed the soap off all the brushes, while I dunked and scrubbed Timmy's tail in the bucket.

When the pony was all clean and rinsed, I scraped excess water from his coat and untied him. Clara and I led him up the bare hill behind the house so he could pick around the sagebrush for some grass while he dried.

"Mum, look at his pastern," she said. "It looks so much better! I can't believe it."

"I know. I'm amazed," I said. "'Time heals all wounds.'"

"Time didn't heal it," she said. "Timmy did. And we did." She smiled.

"We had a little bit to do with it," I said, putting my hand on her tiny, bony shoulder blade. "But it does take time. You have to be patient."

Clara held the end of the lead rope loosely, while the

pony pulled at the prickly grass with his muzzle. Timmy was a white pony with brown spots, a Pony of the Americas, but when he was wet you could see another pattern underneath, a different pattern of pink and gray skin that showed only through a wet coat. As he dried in the sun, his clean fur stood out from his skin like velvet and slowly obscured the mottled pattern below.

I sat on the ground and looked down at our house. The roof needed work and there was no plan to the landscaping. Well, there was no landscaping, it was just the way it had always been, and it looked pretty shabby. But as I sat there with Clara, I realized how much I cared for it. It didn't have a "magazine-quality kitchen" like I read about in real estate ads, and there was no magnificent fireplace, no "storage galore," but it was home.

I turned to Clara and said, "I just can't believe you're going to be seven!"

She beamed, looked up at me, and then she turned toward a rattling-rumble sound on Bear Creek Road in front of our house.

"Daddy!" she screamed and started tearing down the hill, dropping Timmy's rope to the ground and not worrying about it one bit.

George's truck pulled slowly into the driveway and stopped under the silver poplar tree by the house. He beeped the horn and waved a tan arm out the window.

I pulled a reluctant Timmy behind me down the hill as George and Clara hugged each other, jumping up and down.

He was taller than I remembered and his teeth whiter. God, he looked so good, standing there in his white shirt and Levi's.

He hugged me and whirled me around with ease, as if I were a little person, which I'm not. He stopped when he realized we were getting tangled in Timmy's lead rope. I remember Clara laughing and clapping her little dirty hands.

"Let me get a look at you," George said, stepping back. "God, you are two beautiful girls!"

For a moment, all my anguish and anxiety, and all my questions, melted away. My mind stayed right where it should. George was home. The three of us were together again.

chapter 30

In the heat of the afternoon, George unloaded his truck, making trip after trip down the cellar stairs with equipment.

I carried his two nylon black duffel bags up onto the front porch and started going through his things. Shaving kit inside on the stairs to be taken up by whoever passed that way next, books and stray papers on the dining room table for him to sort out later, and three piles of clothes: darks, lights, and so dirty they'd better be washed twice. I added Clara's and my laundry to the piles, and the cover of Percy's dog bed went in the double-wash pile. Clara found an old towel to cover the dog bed with in the meantime; God forbid Percy didn't have his bed for a moment.

As I dumped each group of clothes into big black garbage bags, George walked by with a load of equipment in his hands.

"What are you doing with all that?" he asked.

"Washing machine's broke," I said, imitating my favorite colloquial use of the English language.

"Broke?" he said.

"Broke," I said. "Dryer's broke, too. Gotta go to the Laund-Ra-Matt."

"That's great!" he teased. "You love that place, and while the clothes are washing you could always go next door and look around Howell's."

Howell's is the biggest of Hayden's many pawnshops.

Then, at the same time, the Howell's Pawnshop motto came out of both of our mouths: "Pawn in Private. Ladies Welcome."

"Everything's falling apart," he said with a smile. "Did you see the tire on my truck?"

I hadn't.

"It's got a slow leak. I must have driven over a nail or something. I'm just glad I made it home without having to change to that skinny spare—I hate those things." He pulled the screen door open. "Do we have any beer?" he asked.

"I think so."

He went into the house and came out carrying two beers and a rickety old chair.

"Will you sit and talk to me while I get that tire off?"

I set the chair under the silver poplar. George opened the bottles and handed one to me. We clinked bottles, kissed each other quickly, and drank. When George tipped his bottle the second time, I watched his Adam's apple to be sure he drank. He did.

We decided he'd take the tire off and I could take it in to be fixed the next day on my way to the Nicholsons' ranch with Timmy.

He set the brake, pulled the jack out from under the hood, and went to work lifting the truck up, and all the while he chatted. I knew he must have missed me because normally if he's working on something he doesn't say anything, even if he tells me he wants my company while he gets whatever it is done. Usually he just works; he forgets about the talking part.

Clara played around by the truck, sometimes listening to us. The afternoon melted into evening, and the harsh summer light softened to a slanted glow. George talked and talked.

Of course, I hadn't managed to pull together an elaborate plan for a beautiful welcome home dinner, so we had spaghetti with regular old sauce from a jar and Parmesan cheese. George mounded his plate high and ate every bite. He and Clara had a spaghetti-slurping

contest, and the evening passed in relaxed content-
edness. George's return was as sweet as any I could
remember.

My worries about Tom would have to wait for another
day.

chapter 31

Clara's big day finally arrived. At first her excitement was
endearing when she came bounding into our room just
after first light, jumping up and down in innocent delight.
She climbed into bed with George and me and wriggled
around like a smiling jumping bean. Then she escaped
from under the covers, shrieking and running about with
her light brown hair flying. At that point her expression
began to verge on an obsessed look and her skinny ex-
tremities seemed to move beyond her control. Her day
was upon her, the day she'd been talking and dreaming
about for months, and it was as if she was determined to
make it a different kind of day, by sheer force of energy,
if necessary. She was a beautiful example of frenzied excitement teetering right on the edge of anger and disappointment. And by eight o'clock in the morning she was
already driving me crazy. My pleasure in dropping her off
for a few hours at Casey Williamson's hunkered-down
house made me think I must be some kind of coldhearted

woman. I drove home feeling nervous, jigged-up, as my grandfather used to say. I was also annoyed with myself for being rushed and disorganized on her birthday, and somewhere near the surface was a sense of dread—dread about the party, dread about Tom.

I returned from leaving Clara with Casey to make a phone call and to wrap the Barbie and the things I'd ordered from catalogs—baking clay and two books. I went to the basement to get the wrapping paper and ribbon and the cheapo, pink paper tablecloth, party hats, and pin-the-tail-on-the-donkey, all from Party Central on the Boardwalk by Wal-Mart. George was in his office, tipped back in his chair, leisurely looking through papers on his desk. He waved to me and I went about my business, wondering how he could be so relaxed when we had a birthday party to pull together.

As I cut and taped and tied, my head felt like it had a thousand voices debating within. With the last piece of ribbon scraped into a curl by the blade of the scissors, I marched back down the still grubby basement stairs, heart pounding and palms sweating.

"George," I said. He was now in the wood shop pulling the blanket off Clara's desk. "I have to talk to you."

He looked up seriously, and in the dim light of the basement his face looked paler than the day before, and tired.

"OK," he said.

"I've got something to tell you." My voice shook in my throat.

"What is it?" He almost looked afraid, like he was mentally bracing himself. It was the kind of look I imagine a husband might give a wife when he knows she's about to tell him there has been someone else.

"It's about Tom," I said. "Tom Baxter. Your mother's friend."

"I know who you mean," he said. George's head was perfectly still. "What is it?"

"I don't think he's who he says he is," I said.

"OK," George said, and I'm sure a flood of possibilities ran quickly through his mind.

I took a deep breath and looked George square in the eyes. "I think Tom is Whitey Bulger."

With that everything changed. George's face came immediately alive; he tipped his head all the way back and exploded in howling laughter!

"Really?!" he said, not even trying to contain his laughter. "You think Whitey Bulger, wanted by the FBI, is dating my mother?"

"I do," I said seriously. I wanted to slap him.

"This is fabulous," he said, not even noticing how I was seething. "Isn't he a murderer? And like some kind of Irish Mafia boss? The guy you and Joanie babble on about all the time?" I don't think it ever crossed George's mind that I might possibly be serious. Nothing came out of my mouth. Never did I even imagine this type of response from him was a possibility.

"This is great! I love it. Lorraine Colter finally has a boyfriend and it's Whitey Bulger!"

He was still so wrapped up in the humor of it all that he didn't even notice my tears, which had started out of frustration.

"You're an asshole!" I must have screamed. I'd never said anything like that to George before. Never.

He snapped to and said, "Wait a minute. You're serious?" He shook his head in disbelief. "You can't be serious, Kate."

"Yes, I *am* serious. And you have no idea what's been going on here—what I've been worrying about—for the last three weeks!" I shouted. "Forget it. Just forget it. You're a jerk, you know it? A jerk."

I turned to go back upstairs.

"No. Wait," he said, grabbing me by the elbow. "Come back. Here, sit down and tell me."

I turned around but was too worked up to sit down. I didn't feel like telling him anything by then.

"C'mon, tell me," he pleaded. His face was serious.

"I don't know," I said. "I don't really want to talk about it now."

"Kate, I'm sorry. I had no idea. I really thought you were joking. What's going on?"

"OK," I said, but I didn't know where to begin. George didn't say any more that I remember. I think he just listened, both of us standing in the cool of the basement. I started in something like this: "Well, you know I really like Tom. That day at the parade, when we first met him, I felt like he was someone I wanted to get to know better. I was excited he was in Hayden. Do you know what it's like for me here when you're away? I don't know if you do. But when I met Tom and the more I've spent time with him this summer, the more I've realized how different it is here—how alone I am. I mean I have you and I have Clara and there's nothing like that. This is my home. But still I'm alone. Tom knows about things and he *talks* and he tells stories and the conversation just flows easily from one thing to another. He has real conversations. Right from the beginning I knew I liked him and for some reason I felt a connection. There's something about him that makes me feel at home. He reminds me of things and people who are familiar, of people like me, or of my family that's gone. But then there were weird things, like that night we went to the rodeo with Robbie and Janna. I don't think I ever mentioned it to you, but when I saw Tom there, he crossed himself. He had a strange expression on his face ..."

I went on talking to George for a while. I told him about the way Tom said "yeste'day" at Shipton's, how he returned my watch and said he wondered how observant I was, and how he likes dogs, how we ran into him at the Custer Battlefield and he took Lorraine to Fort Johnson. He borrowed a book from me. I told him about the librarian and the "regular older man" asking about the *Boston Globe*. George was trying to understand, to redeem himself with me in some way, but I could tell underneath, he wasn't buying my theory.

"OK." I paused for a minute, collecting my thoughts. "I saw him cross himself at the rodeo. He had a tight, hard look on his face. At the Custer Battlefield I asked him if he was Catholic. He said he wasn't."

George raised his eyebrows. Then I told him all about the meeting at the bar and what Tom had told me about becoming a priest.

"Well," George said, as if Tom's story might explain it all.

"Well, that's not all. I made a phone call this morning to St. John's Seminary in Brighton, Massachusetts. Tom said he went there. They have no record of a Tom Baxter ever going there."

"Really?" George asked.

"No Tom Baxter. George, I'm telling you, he's Whitey Bulger."

George sat down on the edge of Clara's new desk. He looked down and then with both hands began slowly rubbing his temples.

"Kate, he may not be who he says he is," he said calmly, "or his past might be shady, I don't know, but, God, he's not Whitey Bulger."

"I think he is," I said.

"You know what I think," he said, pulling me toward him like he wanted to kiss me, and maybe even change the subject. "I think maybe you were just bored with me away, so you cooked this all up to entertain yourself."

That did it. I was furious.

"That's not fair! I'm serious, George," I said. "Jesus!"

I turned to leave.

"Kate, for God's sake, be reasonable."

"Reasonable?" I chided. "What's reasonable?"

"Not this! This is ridiculous!" Now he was mad, too.

"But you know what pisses me off?" George's eyes narrowed. "If you really think, which I do *not*, that this guy is Whitey Bulger—a murderer, probably armed and dangerous—what are you doing? What the hell are you doing? Why haven't you said anything?" He turned to walk back into the shop. Then spun toward me again on his heel. "And why the frick aren't you one bit worried about my mother? She's the one who would be in danger!"

"I was waiting for you! I thought you'd help me—you'd know what to do. But forget it! Just forget it!" I stormed up the stairs and out into the sunlight.

Not only was I mad, I was also a nervous wreck. I'd bided my time waiting for George to come home. And it had gone all wrong, not how I expected at all. All wrong. He pissed me off with his patronizing way and also because part of me knew he was right. It was unlikely, but more than that, if Tom was Whitey Bulger, why was I thinking only of Tom and myself? I had thought of Lorraine, but not enough the way I should have.

Tom would be coming to the party and maybe George would see what I meant. Regardless of how badly our conversation had gone, I knew George would be unable to look at Tom without thinking of my suspicions.

I did a few things around the barn and then went to pick Clara up from Casey's. It's a short drive up the road, so we were home quickly, just enough time for Clara to eat a banana. I drove past the house and up the slight rise to the barn, looping out to the east so I could pull up in front of the horse trailer with the truck facing out. The smell of crushed sagebrush came in through open windows as we drove off the beaten path.

Clara's seat belt was off and she perched herself at the front of the bench, her little hands on the dusty dashboard. She bounced up and down on the tan vinyl, singing, "Five more hours till my party ... five more hours till my party ..."

I stopped in front of the trailer and she jumped out almost instinctively, running behind to get ready for her position on top of the trailer tongue. She waited while I spun the crank five times, lifting the hitch above the ball on the truck. I walked back to the cab of the truck; she climbed up on the tongue and held her hand high, right in line with the hitch. With her other hand she directed me, pointing left and right: "A little more ... that's good ... slow ... stop!"

We had a pretty good system, she and I, for getting the ball right under the hitch. When she said stop, I put the truck in park and came back to check. We were right on. Sometimes things went well. Clara cranked the hitch onto the ball (it's easier on the way down), while I plugged in the power cable and secured the safety hooks.

I pulled the trailer around to the front of the barn and the two of us swept it out and hosed it down. There would be enough time for it to dry before we loaded Timmy up for the trip home. I thought George would come out to see us, but there was no sign of him coming from the house. In fact, I thought I heard a hum of tools coming from the basement. I thought that part of Clara's desk was all done—hadn't he varnished it already? So why did he choose this morning to saw, or router, or power-sand? Wouldn't he rather be with us?

Clara played with the hose in the dust. I went in to the barn to fill a hay net so Timmy would have something to occupy him on the ride. When I came out I saw a car had pulled up behind George's jacked-up truck. It was a blue sedan I didn't recognize. Then I saw someone headed toward the front porch. It was Tom Baxter. He had something in his hand. Then from where I was by the barn, he was out of my sight.

What was going on? Why was he here so early?

"I'll be right back, honey," I said to Clara, who was so busy with the hose, she hadn't noticed the car drive in.

I walked quickly for the back door. My mind raced, and I felt a vague internal shaking. Why was Tom here? How would I face him? How would I act with Tom in front of George, who knew my suspicions? I felt exposed and somehow hypocritical and I wasn't ready yet. I didn't know enough.

When I was nearly to the house, I heard a sound I hope I never hear again as long as I live. A scream, of sorts, but more like a high-pitched, loud human intake of air.

Then there was the sound of commotion and men's intermingled voices. *Oh shit . . . Fuck . . . God no . . . Shit.*

I ran for the kitchen, scrambling up the back steps and

through the screen door. The scream turned to moaning, but I couldn't see much with eyes accustomed to the sharp brightness of the sun. Things started coming into focus, and out of my visual darkness I could see Tom with his arms around a nearly collapsed George. There was blood everywhere—bright streaks on the walls by the basement stairs, all over Tom and George, and in pools on the linoleum floor. Tom looked stunned, and there was my beautiful, strong George as helpless as a maimed deer, inconceivably reduced by pain and confusion.

I wanted to kill Tom right then and there. I wished I had a metal cable with which to snap his neck. I wanted to stomp his head into the ground. Everything whirled around me, lights and colors and sounds, like a Las Vegas casino. Then out of the swirling mess, I began to hear Tom's voice yelling to me, "Kate! Pull yourself together! Get me a rope or an extension cord!"

What? What was he saying?

"Anything, Kate! Rip up a sheet? I've got to get a tourniquet on him! Hurry! He's losing a lot of blood!"

What was happening? I grabbed a dish towel, twisted it, and handed it to Tom. Clara was at the back door. "Daddy! Daddy!" she screeched. "What happened to your hand? Daddy!"

She went to George. I was paralyzed. What had happened? I didn't reach for Clara. I didn't go to George.

I don't think I said a thing. I just stood there uselessly leaning against the counter.

"He got his hand caught in the table saw," Tom said to Clara calmly. "It's OK, honey."

He looked up at me. "I don't know if he's got any fingers left. Maybe one. Get me a towel to wrap this in."

It was only then that I began to concentrate on the sight before me. Tom tied the strip of dish towel tightly just above George's elbow, and hanging limp at the end of the arm was a ragged mess of blood, skin, flesh, and bones. It looked like unevenly ground stew beef mixed with chunks and shards of white bone and tan skin—dark, thick-looking red blood, darker than I'd ever seen, pulsed from the depths of the serrated human pulp. Nothing was recognizable to me until almost as high as the wrist.

All at once voices surrounded my head.

"Daddy!" Clara cried.

"Kate!" Tom shouted. "Jesus, Kate! C'mon! Get your car! You have to take him to the hospital. Now!"

"Nine-one-one!" Clara yelled. "Call nine-one-one!"

"No!" Tom said. "It'll take too long. Kate! Get moving."

Clara picked up the phone anyway. How many times had we told her, If there's an emergency call 911. If you feel funny, running out of steam, and for some weird reason you can't find Mom or Dad, or you're at someone else's house, don't wait. Call 911.

"Mummy, the phone doesn't work."

For no reason at all that statement gave me a clear thought: The phone doesn't work because the battery's finally dead. I never got a new one.

"Oh, George," I gasped as I turned toward the back door. "Shit! My truck's got the trailer and George's is up on the jack."

"Damn it!" Tom shouted. "Damn it!" He pursed his lips and shook his head. There was the hard expression again. "I'll have to take you."

Tom, who never really seemed out of sorts, who could clearly handle all the blood and gore, helped George to the car. I put my arms around Clara. I was coming out of my stupor. The facts came together slower than they should have. George caught his hand in the goddamned table saw. Tom didn't do this to him, he did it to himself. Shit!

"Clara, you get in the front," Tom said. "Let your mom and dad have the back."

"I'm not allowed in the front seat," said Clara, sounding afraid.

"Get in the front seat." Tom raised his voice, but not too much.

Clara looked up at me, wondering what to do. I nodded and opened the passenger side door for her.

Tom hoisted George into the back and I ran around to climb in the other side. He put George's arm in my lap and put my hands tightly around the towel that now wrapped the mangled hand. Blood seeped all the way through the layers of pink terry cloth.

"Just hold it tight," Tom said.

We backed out onto Bear Creek Road. Tom slammed the transmission into drive and floored it. The tires spun on the dirt and red shale road.

George slumped against me. He was losing color and I thought maybe consciousness, too, but the moaning never stopped. It was almost rhythmic and obviously involuntary. He sounded like a very, very sick little child.

I could just see the top of Clara's small head. It was pressed back against the seat, and her hand held the armrest tightly. She neither cried, nor spoke, nor looked back at her suffering father.

Heavier and heavier was the weight of George's arm in my lap and of his body leaning against me.

"Will my daddy be OK?" Clara asked of no one in particular. She didn't get an answer.

We passed the Williamsons' house at great speed and then turned and headed for town on the long empty stretch of County Road 64. Tom's eyes were fixed ahead.

Between George's moans, I thought I could hear Tom

muttering. The back of his cowboy hat moved slightly from side to side, as if he were shaking his head and saying no to himself.

Then somewhere along 64 a single car passed us going the other direction, headed toward Bear Creek Road. It was a sheriff's Blazer, and not surprisingly, because that's what the sheriff does most of the time, drives the back county roads. Of course, I wondered if he would turn around and stop us for speeding. Tom never slowed, or turned his head to look at the cruiser; he just kept going, repeatedly staring in the rearview mirror until the sheriff was out of sight. I watched as his eyes filled with something. It wasn't fear and it wasn't anger. I can only describe it as hate.

Brave little Clara turned and looked up at him. "How long till we get there, Mr. Baxter?"

"Shut up!" he shot back at her, his eyes moving up and down between the dirt road ahead and the rearview mirror. It was then that he must have realized I'd been studying him from the backseat. Our eyes locked in the mirror, and for a few moments time stood still. I could see it and he could see it—there was no question. Because of an image in a backward-looking mirror, he knew right then for certain that I knew. And I knew more about him than he could allow.

The car swerved suddenly to the right. George and I

nearly slid off the backseat as we came to a skidding stop. A small noise, like a high-pitched animal wail, came from Clara in the front. Then as quick as a cat on a mouse, Tom sprang at her. He turned sideways toward the back of the car with Clara in a headlock, her throat virtually throttled in the crook of his right elbow.

"Get out of my car," he said in a low voice.

And there it was, in his left hand, the pearl-handled jackknife.

"No!" I yelled, reaching toward Clara. "Tom! No! What are you doing?"

He pulled back, out of my reach, and under his breath said, "I can't believe you got me into this shit. Jesus Fucking Christ. Get out!"

The blade was near her face. Clara made no sound, but tears sprang from her tightly closed eyes.

"Tom! Stop!" I pleaded. "Help us, please."

"I mean it. Get the fuck out of my car! Both of you."

I don't think George ever knew what was happening. His moaning kept on.

"I can't!" I said. "Please don't hurt my baby!"

"Out, now!" He pulled Clara up even tighter against his chest.

It was the worst moment of my life.

"You get out of my car and I'll let her go," he said. "Get out." His eyes were ice blue and haunted.

What the hell do you do?

In a split second my mind created newspapers spinning toward me, like in the old movies. Headlines like "Child Stabbed by Fugitive" and "Family Found Dead on County Road 64" came into focus. I thought of the old grandmother's last living moment in the ditch on the side of the road in Flannery O'Connor's "A Good Man Is Hard to Find." The old lady talked and talked at The Misfit, an escaped convict, until he shut her up with three bullets in the chest.

Then suddenly, I was surprisingly calm. Strangely calm. I even remember reminding myself, This is really happening to you right now. This is not something you're imagining or reading about. This is real.

And then I did it—the practically unimaginable. I looked at Clara's sweet face and the silver blade by her plump cheek. I took a good look at Tom. I opened the door over George and slowly pushed him from the car.

"Mummy, no," Clara whimpered from Tom's hold. "Mummmmmmmy."

George crumpled onto the dust. I climbed out after and closed the back car door. Steady and deliberate were my motions. Slowly, I turned back toward the car. I was out. And my little girl was in—with him.

It was as if each moment, each decision, each movement, all of it clicked by in slow motion, and then in an instant everything flipped to fast forward. The passenger side door flew open. Little Clara came tumbling out in a heap onto the dirt. The car and the man went racing off, spraying dirt and shale over the three of us.

chapter 32

There we were, George, Clara, and I, on the side of the road.

A meadowlark sat on a fencepost nearby singing over and over again his unforgettable melody. How eerie it was to have in my ears the thrilling birdsong of the West and in my eyes a beaten and bloody family, my family. Miles ahead in the distance, the dust cloud thrown by Tom Baxter's car turned south, away from Hayden. In that direction the dirt road heads for one place, the Becket entrance to the interstate.

The midday sun beat down with force over the vast landscape. Dusty-looking greenish-gray swells, cut by a few tightly strung barbed-wire fences, extended in all directions. The occasional cottonwood hung on at the bottom of a draw. To the west in the distance, Black Angus sparsely dotted a hillside. The only signs of humanity were fences, the dry road, and miles of telephone poles strung with swooping wires.

George lay on his side in the long brittle grass that sloped down toward the ditch beside the road. With his good hand he held his wrist and pressed the bloody towel against his chest. The noise that came from him was a soft, drawn-out agony. Clara stood over him with two dirty skinned knees and elbows, her face streaked with tears and dirt. I went to each of them, hugging them. Then I stomped my anger out marching tight circles on the road.

Clara or I could begin walking and the other wait with George, but she was unquestionably too little for either job alone. So we did the only thing we could do—we waited. I wondered how long George would last; I tried to figure out how long ago it was that Clara ate the banana in the truck. For how long we waited, I don't have any idea. Twenty minutes, two hours, it was all distorted by pain, worry, and thirst. All I know is all that matters; George survived the wait and so did Clara.

Eventually a young man, maybe twenty years old, came along in a pickup. He began slowing to a stop even before I flagged him. The three of us squeezed into the cab with him, George a human heap. I said we needed to go to the hospital and he nodded and said, "Yes, ma'am, looks like you do." He had an open can of Coke in the cup holder, and I asked if Clara could have a sip or two. He said, "Sure, have the rest." He asked no questions and we asked none of him.

chapter 33

My memories of the hospital are strange and blurred. I'd imagined myself there a hundred times, but always in my mind I was there for an emergency situation with Clara, never for George. Nurses and doctors rushing out from stations and offices off the hall as they became alerted to George's arrival. George taken away around a corner to a room made by hanging curtains. Clara and I shepherded to a mauve and gray room to answer questions from a woman with a long, pink face. She talked without ever looking away from her computer screen.

"His name ... date of birth ... social security number ... still live on Bear Crik? ... still employed out at the college? ... religious affiliation ..."

My answers were one word, whenever possible, and with no humanlike responses from Pink Face, I looked around the barren, windowless room until my eyes landed unfocused on the Patients' Bill of Rights. It was like visual stumbling, eyes moving from the oak veneered desk, to the empty in and out boxes, to the Hayden Insurance cardboard tent calendar, to the sign of a cigarette with a line through it, until at last my vision rested on words, uninteresting and virtually unintelligible, but at least the Patients' Bill of Rights had a lot of words.

Clara stood next to my oak and mauve chair, leaning into me, her arm over my shoulder and her fingers twirling the hair at the nape of my neck.

We moved from there to a waiting room. Before I sat down, I got a bag of cookies for Clara from the vending machine and called Lorraine from the pay phone in the corner. She wasn't home. George, we were told, had been taken to surgery. Did I worry whether the surgeon would be good enough, or whether George was in the right hands? No. I didn't. I was numb, "calm of mind, all passion spent."

Clara and I sat, silent mostly, in a dreary waiting room. People must have come in and out, but I don't remember them. I do remember looking down at the back of my left hand. With the nail of my right forefinger I haphazardly picked at the dried blood between my fingers. My hand looked old. The skin was cracked and lined, dirty and bloody, but mostly it was old. The hairs on my arm stood out from goose-bumped skin. Dried sweat, caked blood, and dirt did little to keep me warm in the much too air-conditioned hospital.

Clara shivered and snuggled closer to me.

"It's my birthday, Mummy," she said very quietly. There was no whine to her voice.

Tears slid silently down my cheeks. The taste of salt mixed with dirt on my chapped lips.

"I know, sweetheart." That was all I could muster the strength to say and still hold it together.

I thought of the three little presents wrapped and sitting on our dining room table. And the party hats and tablecloth left in a pile. The bag of balloons hadn't been blown up. The table wasn't set. And the cake. God, the cake! All she wanted was a pink and white cake, and I didn't even get that for her. It wasn't waiting for her at home.

Time passed and a doctor came out to talk to me, still in his surgical scrubs. He looked younger than I. Clara listened to everything he said probably better than I did.

"He's stable," the doctor said. "Everything went as well as it could."

I must have been like a zombie.

"We lost three fingers and a portion of a fourth," he said. "But I think we were able to save the hand."

I nodded, not really thinking about it, my eyes unable to focus on anything.

"You can see him in a few minutes. A nurse will come get you."

I sat back down gingerly, lowering myself into the chair like an old person. Clara climbed up on my lap. I rested my chin on the back of her shoulder.

Then the tinted sliding doors to the outside opened. And there came a vision of pink splendor, a quick-stepping Lorraine. Hooked around one wrist was an enormous bunch of pink and purple balloons. From the other arm hung a shopping bag with the top of a package and elaborately curled metallic ribbons poking out the top. And in her hands was a gorgeous pink and white birthday cake.

Her voice shattered the quiet of the emergency waiting room.

"Where's Grammy's birthday girl?" In her bright smile was total, uncomplicated affection. "Isn't it someone's birthday today?"

Clara leaped from my lap.

"Grammy!" She ran toward Lorraine, arms outstretched.

"Oh, honey, don't knock Grammy over! See, I've got the cake in my hand, sweetheart." She looked around. "Let me find somewhere to put this down."

She put it all on the coffee table and stood up straight, wiping the sweat from her brow.

"Nice and cool in here."

"Oh, Lorraine!" I went to her and nearly collapsed

on her little frame. She felt sturdy and solid. "Oh, thank you."

I gulped for air and still couldn't catch my breath.

Lorraine put her arms gently around me, patting my back.

"George ..." I managed to gasp.

"I know, honey. I know all about it. You don't have to tell me." Her voice was comforting.

"How did you know? I tried to call, but ..."

"Oh, Dalene got me. I couldn't imagine what she would be calling about; you know she hasn't called for years and years." Lorraine ran her hand across the back of her neck. "Anyway, she said you were up at the hospital. You know her daughter-in-law, Kristi, works here now. Evidently, she called Dalene to say George had come in."

"It's so awful," I cried. "All of it. The whole thing. It's just so awful."

"Yes, honey, it is." She put her arms around me again. "It is just pitiful." Then she whispered in my ear, "Now you get ahold of yourself, honey. It's time. You can do it."

She stepped back and turned to Clara. "Who wants some birthday cake? C'mon over here and give me a hug, you big seven-year-old girl!"

Clara hugged Lorraine around the middle. Lorraine

reached down and put her long smooth fingers, bright with pink nail polish to match her lipstick, under Clara's chin, and lifted the little face to look up.

"Bet you'd like a present, too, sweetheart," she said, pulling a package from her bag.

"Oh, Grammy, thank you!"

Thank you, Lorraine. Thank you indeed!

chapter 34

I went in to see George first. He was groggy and as white as a sheet, almost green under the fluorescent lights. I hugged him and told him how I loved him. I assured him that we were all safe and we all had made it. He nodded and turned his face into my neck as I bent over the bed. Clara came to his bedside and he managed to move his head to the side of the mattress and kiss her cheek. Straining, he even forced his mouth in a quasi-smile for her.

Then Lorraine entered, smelling of powder and perfume, and George dissolved. There was his mother, standing tall, fresh, and clean in the midst of catastrophe. His face remained strangely expressionless from the drugs, but all the bravery he'd summoned fell away in the presence of his mother.

When Clara and I got home it was dark. Percy met us at the door, and I remembered that Timmy was still in his stall. The Nicholsons' grandchildren must have had a disappointing day.

On the dining room table, next to the party hats, there were three things that caught my eye—an envelope on top of a small wrapped package on top of a book. The book was the Sitting Bull biography, *The Lance and the Shield*, that Tom had borrowed. He must have left it all on the table when he heard George's gasp. The package was wrapped in paper with little pink roses all over it and was clearly for Clara. She opened the tiny box, and there was a silver chain with a tiny silver shamrock pendant. Two names were written across the front of the envelope in bold capital letters: KATE AND GEORGE. I muddled my way through opening the envelope, making a ragged tear across the top. Inside was a small note on plain white paper.

Dear Kate and George:

Please tell Clara I'm sorry I missed her party. I hope she likes the necklace.

Some things have come up and I have to leave Hayden sooner than I expected. Take care, Tom.

P. S. New Maytag washer and dryer waiting for you to pick up at Sears. All paid for.

chapter 35

A little more than a year has passed since that awful day. Clara is now eight years old.

What I've spent so much of my time worrying about, planning for, trying to prevent, wasn't it at all. Clara's little body didn't run out of steam. I didn't make a huge mistake that allowed her to go for too long without food. No, it wasn't an MCADD seizure that nearly destroyed our family last year, it was a pearl-handled knife.

George has had two more operations, both in Denver, and he's doing as well as can be expected with his mangled, mostly fingerless hand. With mock affection he refers to it as "The Claw." He even worked out a system to finish the thresholds. I found out later it was wood for the thresholds, which I'd nagged him about for years, that George was sawing the day of the accident. How typical of him to start a project like that at such an odd time, a wrong time really, and even more like him to fight with me and then immediately get to work on something *for* me.

He thinks he can still feel his missing fingers and he dreams about them. I'm sure he grieves over the hand that was destroyed, too. He must, though he never says. Not surprisingly, he's still much more interested in fifty-million-year-old fish, *Knightia* and *Priscacara*, than in his own hand. The bat George's team found in Kemmerer last summer did turn out to be the oldest bat fossil ever discovered, and from the little guy, *Icaronycteris index*, there's now a clearer picture of the Wyoming environment in the Eocene epoch.

We found out later that Tom told Lorraine just the morning of Clara's birthday that things weren't going to work out between the two of them. It wasn't her, he said, it was him. He told her he really couldn't explain why and she probably wouldn't understand if he did, so he hoped they could just leave it as a happy episode for each of them. He left a pair of diamond earrings she'd admired at Wal-Mart on her kitchen counter and an envelope filled with twenty one-hundred-dollar bills. Among other things, his note to Lorraine said, "I hope you'll make one honey of a money corsage with this." (Lorraine with all her crafty talents can fold dollar bills into a greenback corsage.)

Just before George was released from the hospital, about a week after Clara's birthday, we talked to the Hayden Police and told them everything that happened on County Road 64. We gave a physical description of Tom and told them all we could remember about the blue car he was driving. I didn't say anything about Tom possibly being Whitey Bulger—I just couldn't—and I knew the officer wouldn't get it anyway. I thought George might say something, since I was sure he realized I was right by then. But he didn't, either. I guess neither one of us felt it was our duty to do the job for the police.

I told Lorraine of my suspicions about Tom one day last fall and she said, "Serious?" She was silent for a moment and then said, "No, honey, I don't think you're right. Tom was a good man and he sure liked you. Something's just not right with him and I don't understand it. But, I'll tell you what, I'll never forgive a man who did what he did to George. And to Clara! It just makes me sick. Nope. I can never forgive him for that." She put her hands up to her earlobes. "I have a hard time wearing these earrings because of it, too. But then I think what good does not wearing 'em do. He's gone and they're here. And aren't they gorgeous!"

Lorraine thought I was all wrong about Tom until two clean-cut FBI agents showed up at her door.

They asked a lot of questions, but nothing surprising. "Where did you meet Tom Baxter? What did he tell you about his past? Did he talk about being in touch with anyone? Did you ever see him use money?" They asked me all about the day at the Custer Battlefield. They had a tip about that day, but didn't move on it quickly because, believe it or not, there are a lot of "Whitey Sightings." A woman did notice him and his companions, me and Clara, buying a doll at the register at the Trading Post.

Then they showed us a picture and asked, "Is this Tom Baxter?" It unquestionably was. I said yes and returned with a question. "Is that a picture of James Bulger?"

The one who seemed to be in charge looked at the other agent, then back at me, and nodded his head. They told us no more.

"Where's Whitey?" is still the question, but really only in Boston. After the FBI visit I decided to tell Joanie the whole story. She was shocked by it all. I remember her saying, "Here I was in my office picturing you with the cows and hay, bored out of your mind, and that's what was going on! Jesus Christ!"

I was relieved that Joanie wasn't the least bit bothered by the fact that I had kept all of it from her for so long. It might have been because by then she had met Michael. Michael O'Connor is crazy about Joanie and, guess what, she's crazy about him. They met late last summer and, shock of all shocks, it was good old Swivel Elf who introduced them. Hard to believe but true. Swivel Elf came through in the end. Swiv talked to Michael in a long line at Borders one lunch hour, and on a lark she told him he should meet her boss. He said fine, tell him when and where and he'd be there. So Swiv took the bull by the horns and made the lunch reservation and sent them both off to meet each other.

Anyway, one thing Joanie said on the phone the day I told her all that had happened, I'll never forget.

I said something like, "In so many ways I liked him. I really did. Can you believe it, Whitey Bulger? I was with Whitey Bulger! There I was in the car with a murderer."

Joanie was serious, no joking at all, and she said, "You don't know that for sure."

"Joanie, I KNOW he was Whitey!"

"Not that part. That's not what I'm talking about," she said. "Remember, Kate, this is America—innocent until proven guilty. Alleged murderer. He's been indicted on racketeering charges and drug dealing and murder, but innocent until proven guilty. We don't know. And Jesus, who the hell knows, that fricking *Boston Globe* is so slanted, who knows what's true. Until he's brought to trial, all you really know for certain is what happened to you. What he did to George and Clara. And to you."

chapter 36

And I guess that's it. Here I am a year later, and I realize that all we really know without a doubt is ourselves. I'm reminded of something I read that Wallace Stegner wrote near the end of his life: "The only earth I know is the one I have lived on, the only human experience I am at all sure of is my own." I remember reading that years ago and thinking, Oh, isn't that interesting, how true, so right he is, but I didn't understand him, I didn't really get it at all. I'm just beginning to comprehend now, and I'll try to understand better the more I live.

I don't know what Clara's seventh birthday did to her. How did it change her to see her father mangled, bloody, and helpless, to have someone turn on her so completely as Tom did, and to have a knife threatening her young life? I suspect she'll be all right. I see strength in the way she holds her shoulders and softness in the way she still plays like a little girl with Percy. Yet I don't know.

You can plan, and prepare, and protect, but in the end you can't really know what it is that you need to plan, and prepare, and protect for, or against. You can ask a million questions and carry on countless conversations, and still you don't know. You might have more to think about, and one question, sincerely asked, always leads to another. Human nature is curious and should overcome complacency and apathy and avoid the seduction of lazy entertainment. But you can live with someone day in and day out and miss what's important. You can go through something with somebody, even someone you love, and see what happened, but you can't really know what it means for them. We have to be curious, we have to ask, we have to remember, we have to talk, we have to learn, and we have to try. But we also have to remember, in this life, you just never know.

More than ten years have passed. James J. "Whitey" Bulger is still out there and he's still very much a wanted man. In fact, he's just below Osama Bin Laden on the FBI's Ten Most Wanted List. The world has changed, and now with the Internet, anyone anywhere can find out about the Bulger story in an instant. For a short time we lived the story and it left its mark, so I feel no real need to follow it until they find him, if they find him. The James Bulger we knew, Tom Baxter, has never made any contact again whatsoever with George, me, Clara, or Lorraine. As far as I'm concerned, that was probably the last we'll see of him—a trail of dust in the hot, Western, midday sun during the summer of 1995.